Heat Of Battle

"I wouldn't expect someone like you to understand." Anger and agitation built slowly within Laurel. Her head hurt, her eyes burned with unshed tears, and her heart ached as she saw a lifetime of dreams fade away.

"What do you mean, 'someone like me'?"

"A rough, crude sailor with a tattoo on his arm and a woman in every port."

"You left out one thing." John took several steps toward her, his chest almost brushing her breasts.

"What?" Laurel suddenly felt very hot herself as John moved one step closer.

"You're forgetting the worst insult of all."

"The worst insult?" she gasped.

"You haven't called me a damn Yankee, yet."

Dear Reader:

Welcome to Silhouette Desire—sensual, compelling, believable love stories written by and for today's woman. When you open the pages of a Silhouette Desire, you open yourself up to a whole new world— a world of promising passion and endless love.

Each and every Silhouette Desire is a wonderful love story that is both sensuous *and* emotional. You're with the hero and heroine each and every step of the way—from their first meeting, to their first kiss . . . to their happy ending. You'll experience all the deep joys—and occasional tribulations—of falling in love.

This month, look for *Candlelight for Two* by Annette Broadrick, which is the highly anticipated sequel to *A Loving Spirit*. And don't miss Kathleen Korbel's terrific *Man of the Month*, *Hotshot*. Of course, I think every July Silhouette Desire is a winner!

So enjoy . . .

Lucia Macro
Senior Editor

BEVERLY BARTON

YANKEE LOVER

SILHOUETTE *Desire*

Published by Silhouette Books New York

America's Publisher of Contemporary Romance

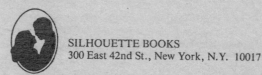

SILHOUETTE BOOKS
300 East 42nd St., New York, N.Y. 10017

ISBN: 0-373-05580-3

First Silhouette Books printing July 1990

BEVERLY BARTON

has been in love with romance since her grandfather gave her an illustrated book of *Beauty and the Beast*. An avid reader since childhood, she took up her own pen at the age of nine and wrote short stories, poetry, plays and novels through high school and college. After marriage to her own "hero" and the births of her daughter and son, she chose to be a full-time homemaker, a.k.a. wife, mother, friend and volunteer.

Six years ago she began substitute teaching and returned to writing as a hobby. In 1987 she joined the RWA and soon afterward helped found the Heart of Dixie chapter in Alabama. Her hobby became an obsession as she devoted more and more time to improving her skills as a writer. Now, her lifelong dream of becoming published has come true.

To Linda Howard
dear friend, mentor and idol!

A special thanks to Celeste Hamilton
for ''everything,''
and Sandra Chastain,
my wonderful Maggie Contest judge

One

The cannon blast boomed through the loud din of festival noises at the exact moment the sound of splashing water blended with hardy shouts and resounding laughter. John Mason jerked instinctively, then relaxed when he realized the source of the unexpected shot.

Across the road, the Civil War reenactment continued on the west side of Spring Park while John's dark eyes focused on the soaking wet female pulling her glistening body back up on the tiny seat atop the dunking booth. Her modestly cut, one-piece bathing suit did little to conceal the generous curves of her very womanly shape. Slender fingers grabbed long, black hair and gently squeezed out the excess water. John's gaze moved to her oval face, devoid of makeup. *She's beautiful—like a porcelain doll.*

Shaking his head, John forced himself back to reality, wondering if the sweat dotting his forehead was caused by instant lust or the sweltering Alabama June sun. Try as he might, he couldn't take his eyes off the woman's breasts where they swelled invitingly over the top of her sleek purple suit. From the huge crowd gathered around the booth, he knew he wasn't the only male admiring the lady perched high above them all while she smiled, waved, laughed, and dared one and all to try their luck at dunking her.

Against his better judgment, John found himself edging closer and closer to the long line of men who doled out their dollars for a chance to test their pitching skills. He suspected that their ultimate goal was to see this goddess emerge from the water-filled tank.

He decided that since he was here, in the midst of the Helen Keller Festival activities, he might as well enjoy himself. He realized that the idea of finding anyone in this huge crowd was ridiculous. More and more people seemed to be filling the scenic park by the minute. Since he was between jobs, as Gram had pointed out when she'd sent him on this wild-goose chase, he knew that for the first time in his life his time was his own. He couldn't keep from smiling as he remembered how easily his grandmother had dismissed his plans for deep-sea fishing in Florida. She thought her thirty-eight-year-old grandson didn't have anything better to occupy his time than making a detour to some out-of-the-way little town.

"Mercy, Harvey Grimes, you couldn't hit the broadside of a barn with a bazooka," the bathing beauty teased from her perch on the tiny, metal seat. "Why don't you stand back and let one of these men show you how it's done?"

Grinning, Harvey dug into his wallet, pulled out five dollars, and demanded his supply of softballs. "Start saying your prayers, sweetheart. I was just getting warmed up for the kill."

John observed the scene, his own adrenaline pumping overtime as he watched the determined man toss ball after ball without hitting the target. The crowd around the booth grew steadily, but John maintained his place in line. Some primeval macho urge possessed him when he saw old

Harvey finally succeed, his shout of triumph echoing in John's ears.

A small group of teenage girls, clad in bathing suits and shorts, buzzed around the dunking booth, their shrill giggles and flirty poses capturing many a young man's eye. John watched, fascinated by their youth and exuberance, as they chased after stray softballs, tossed out challenges to passersby, and encouraged each patron to try *just one more time.*

Two children with curly blond hair, freckled noses, and huge blue eyes walked into the pitching area, the little boy clutching three softballs in his arms. The girl, a head taller and obviously in charge, took two of the balls and lay them beside her brother. "He's going to throw," she said. "I'm going to watch."

"Special client," the brunette called down to redheaded Jinn Edwards, the teenager in charge of the booth.

Quickly Jinn escorted the little boy to within a foot of the target. He tossed his first ball, but it fell short. His eyes filled with tears, but the bevy of young girls hovered about him with shouts of encouragement. When his second toss barely missed, he grasped the third ball tightly in his tiny fist. After his final toss, there was a moment's hesitation, then the target's catch released, and the mermaid dropped into the tank. The little boy jumped up and down with glee as he shouted, "I did it! I did it!"

Laurel Drew emerged from the water, threw back her head and laughed. "I'll bet you play T-ball," she told the child. "You're a real winner, big boy."

John and every adult in the crowd knew that particular game had been rigged for the child's pleasure, and laughter and congratulatory cheers surrounded the little hero.

One by one, the men and boys gave it their best shot, a few winning, most losing, but all of them enjoying the sport. One teenage boy stood between John and his chance to meet the sultry brunette on her watery dais.

Laurel squirmed on the tiny seat as she waved at Tim, the high school quarterback, who was taking dead aim. Four of his team buddies stood out from the crowd, egging him on with immature innuendos and boyish machismo taunts. Tim swaggered a little as he tossed the ball from hand to hand. He has to impress the girls a little, Laurel thought, amused by the unique mentality of teenage males.

His first shot hit dead center, and Laurel plunged into the refreshingly cool water. From the numerous requests she'd had from customers to take her place in the booth, she realized her enviable position. While everyone else suffered from the oppressive summer heat, she was afforded the luxury of occasional relief.

When Tim's second two shots missed, he ran forward and grabbed one of the softballs before it could be retrieved. Jinn chased him as he ran behind the dunking booth, his buddies joining in the chase, stopping to toss ice from their drink cups at the giggling girls.

Laurel couldn't help giggling, making it very difficult for her to keep a straight face when she yelled down at her playful students. With her best authoritarian schoolteacher voice, she warned. "Enough's enough, kids. Debutantes, we've got customers waiting. You hotshot hunks had better go ride the ponies."

Jinn and her fellow club members shooed the boys away and turned to the next customer.

John handed the redhead his money, and she handed him two softballs. "Good luck, mister."

John placed one ball at his feet, the second filling his steady hand. He'd played skill games before. Twenty years in the Navy, celebrating leave in every port city of the world, had honed his reflexes.

Laurel looked down at the big blond man stepping forward into the pitching area, his huge hand encompassing the softball. She didn't recognize him, but there was no reason why she should. People came from all over the United States to attend this yearly festival in her hometown of Tuscumbia. She thought it odd that this tall, muscular stranger seemed familiar when she was certain that she didn't know him. He wasn't exactly handsome, but he was definitely attractive with an athletic body and sun-bleached hair.

Laurel watched, fascinated as this customer pitched the ball, his biceps bulging beneath his short-sleeved knit shirt. Suddenly the seat gave way beneath her, plunging her into the tank. Emerging from the water, she swung her head from side to side, a spray of moisture circling her. Once seated, she wiped her eyes, stretched her body, and smiled at the dark-eyed man grinning at her.

"Lucky shot," she yelled, her blue violet eyes raking his hard torso from head to toe. "I'll bet you can't do it again."

With enthusiastic shouts from the crowd egging him on, John laughed. "Lady, before I get through with you, you'll think you're a fish."

Even though the blistering noonday sun penetrated the very air she breathed, Laurel felt a chill rack her body. She wasn't sure whether the plunge in the cold water or her unwanted attraction to the stranger caused it. She would not allow herself to become hot and bothered over some man she'd never laid eyes on before. Even if she had known him, she would fight the primitive urges her body had kept under control the last nine years. She would never give another man the chance to humiliate her.

"That's it buddy. Turn 'er into a mermaid." The comment came from a bald, red-faced man in the crowd whose slightly staggering body testified to his inebriated condition.

John's steely glance surveyed the outspoken man, assessed him as a happy drunk, and returned his attention to the woman waiting on her perch. Wet and disheveled, she should have looked uncomfortable and defeated, but not this black-haired beauty. She looked as elegant as a queen on her throne, and as sultry as any man's erotic fantasy. He knew he had to control his own masculine reaction before it embarrassed him.

After the other shot his money afforded him, John stood back, a grin of pure masculine victory on his face as he watched his little fish pull herself up and out of the tank for the second time. He didn't take his eyes off her as she re-seated herself. She looked at him and smiled.

He decided it was time for him to move on. It was past noon, and he was hungry. If he didn't get away from this violet-eyed temptress, he'd be hungry for more than food. He had proved his skill, enjoyed a light flirtation, and devoured her gorgeous body with his eyes until he was on the verge of arousal. Yeah, he damn well knew it was time to move on.

"Scared to try again?"

John's head jerked around. He glared at the teenage girl beside the dunking booth, her bright smile and curly auburn hair singling her out from the group of giggling girls.

He looked from the girl to the woman on the perch. The mermaid was gently shaking her head in a negative gesture and whispering something only the bevy of teenagers could hear.

The little redhead burst into almost hysterical laughter. "Come on, mister, you can buy three balls for two dollars. I'm willing to bet that your luck won't hold out."

John's smile broadened when he saw a challenging gleam in the mermaid's eyes as she wiggled restlessly on the metal seat. "Well, Red, are you in charge of this booth?"

"I'm Jinn Edwards, the club's president." She pointed to the colorfully decorated sign that boldly stated Debutante Club Dunking Booth.

"And just what's a Debutante Club?" he asked.

"It's a high school social club. Ninth graders are rats. Senior girls are the officers. We have to earn our own money to pay for all our club activities, including our big annual dance."

"Isn't she a little old to be a Debutante?" John gestured at the woman who was now glaring down at him. Behind him, the crowd of males waiting for their chance began making impatient noises.

"I'm a former Debutante," Laurel said, wishing this irritating man would go away. She didn't like the fact that he had managed to get under her skin. She never allowed that to happen. Never.

"Well, former Debutante, I'll make you and these club members a deal." Was he out of his mind? He knew better than to make a wager with a lady. Ladies didn't play fair. At least the ones he'd known hadn't.

"What deal?" the little redhead asked, looking from John to her open-mouthed comrades.

"I'll buy the three chances, and if I dunk Miss Former Debutante all three times, she'll have lunch with me." He knew for sure he'd lost his mind. A woman like this meant trouble. He'd steered clear of her kind for fifteen years. If he'd take the time to look around, he was sure to find less threatening entertainment.

"I . . . I . . ." Laurel's stomach twisted into tight knots as she gazed down at the swaggering, overly confident male smiling up at her, challenging her. She hated his type. The ultramasculine Mr. Macho. One of those in a lifetime was one too many. "And if you lose?"

"I'll donate fifty dollars to these girls and wave goodbye." He couldn't understand why he didn't go ahead and do just that. Get away while you can, he told himself. Although he thrived on trouble and had never walked away from a fight in his life, he knew what kind of woman to pursue and what kind to leave alone. Milady on her throne was definitely the kind to avoid.

"Please, Miss Drew," the girls begged in unison. "Please."

Laurel debated, wondering what the odds were that he could dunk her three more times. Surely nobody was that good a shot. It really wouldn't be much of a gamble. But what if he won? Carter had been upset because she'd agreed to give her old high school club an hour of her time. He'd

told her that it was unseemly for a lady of her social standing to flaunt herself half-naked before a bunch of gawking
men. What on earth would he say if she shared lunch with
a perfect stranger?

"You've got a bet." Laurel's smile was at odds with her
feelings of doom. She groaned silently, knowing that somehow she'd probably live to regret her decision. Carter would,
no doubt, have a tantrum, and Aunt Polly would fake a severe case of the vapors.

Laurel braced herself, waiting while the fair-haired
stranger exchanged his money for three softballs. She
watched him intently. He bent down, placing the balls at his
feet, retaining one for the first throw. He tossed the ball into
the air, deftly catching it. Laurel sucked in her breath as she
saw the muscles in his arm flex, then relax as his dark eyes
fixed on the small, round target that activated her seat. It
was not so much that he was tall, or even that he was big.
The rugged strength encompassed in his hard body was what
intimidated Laurel.

Suddenly she noticed a flash of tanned, shapely leg directly behind him. Laurel's eyes moved over and upward
where a tall, shapely blonde stood in a pair of indecently
short shorts and a skimpy halter top. The woman was eye-
ing the stranger like a cat eyes a canary just before swallow-
ing it. Laurel's gaze traveled over the crowd, which now
boasted several who seemed fascinated by the broad-
shouldered man tossing a softball.

"Another hit," Jinn Edwards squealed with laughter as
the crowd roared with approval when Laurel's already damp
body hit the water with a loud splash. "You just might be
lucky enough to lose this bet, Miss Drew."

John rolled the softball around in his hands, hesitating
before taking his next shot. The girls were calling her Miss
Drew. Hell, it couldn't be, he thought. No way. So even if
she isn't Laurel Drew, she could be related to the author of
the newspaper article that was neatly folded in his wallet.
Maybe the local historian who was planning to immortalize

her ancestor in a glowing biography was this bathing beauty's mother or grandmother. He decided that since his purpose here would alienate him from her whole family, his little mermaid wouldn't let him get close enough to her to make a fool of himself.

He'd just throw ball two and not worry about confronting the author of the newspaper article and challenging the story's credibility. Just as he started to pitch, the scantily clad woman behind him moved closer and placed her hand on his shoulder. "Care to make a side bet, honey?"

John's gaze traveled her luscious curves quickly, stopping at the deep cleft between her heavy breasts. She was vulgarly sexy, cheap, and available. John knew her type well. In his younger days, he might have been interested. Unfortunately for him and for Miss Drew, this flashy blonde left him cold. Knowing he'd be better off to take her up on her offer and leave Miss Former Debutante alone, he considered missing the next shot. But one look up at the violet-eyed mermaid sealed his fate.

John turned to the woman beside him and said, "No, thanks." The woman glared at him, and mouthed an obscenity as she stomped away.

Laurel hadn't missed one second of the exchange. She felt nauseated at the thought that with one more hit, she would be sharing lunch with this Neanderthal. Her hands trembled as she clutched the tiny seat beneath her. She'd been a fool to agree to his bet. He was the kind of man who had only one thing on his mind. The only time she'd ever been attracted to his type, she'd come away almost destroyed, her pride shattered and her virginity lost forever.

Laurel wrapped her arms around her stomach and took several deep breaths. She knew what was going to happen. She was actually going to have to eat lunch with him. Well, she'd just have to set him straight right away. She would let him know that she was a lady and already had a gentleman friend. Well, Carter was a gentleman, and he was her friend. And everyone in the county considered them a perfect match

since they were both from good families with similar backgrounds.

The day had started out so perfectly. She'd loved every
minute she'd spent in the dunking booth . . . until now. Just
as she forced an I'm-ready smile on her face, she caught
sight of the man whose presence could rescue her from the
threat of the stranger's magnetism.

"Carter." She yelled his name before thinking how mortified he might be to have her spotlight his presence in the
huge crowd. But she didn't care. If only he'd come over and
stay until the last toss, she could introduce him to her tor-
mentor and suggest the three of them share lunch. Carter
would, of course, be furious, but she would rather endure
his wrath than chance a closer encounter with that . . .
that . . . Yankee.

John glanced around, trying to discern which man was
Carter. Then he noticed a tall, very dignified man step toward the dunking booth. John eyed the other man criti-
cally. A damn pretty boy with a head of thick salt-and-
pepper hair, a neatly trimmed mustache, and an air of old
money that reeked of snobbery. So that's the kind of man
she likes. It figured, John thought. She probably led Mr.
Fancy Pants around by the nose. She was just like another
lady he'd once known. She'd rather settle for safe than to try
to tame a real man.

Laurel didn't like the look on Carter's handsome face.
He'd probably be irritable tonight and ruin all the wonderful plans she'd made for them to share the festivities. Well,
she'd just have to be doubly sweet and apologetic. Carter
never could stay angry with her for long, he was too much
of a gentleman.

Laurel smiled her prettiest Southern belle smile, then blew
Carter a kiss, laughing when she saw a condemning frown
cross his face. She knew she should be ashamed of herself
for deriving so much pleasure from rattling his calm, re-
served demeanor.

"Laurel, dear. Clintelle Simpson will be finishing her turn at the Friends of the Library booth in about ten minutes and suggested that you finish up here and join her." Carter's crystal-blue eyes raked Laurel's wet form. "Surely you've fulfilled your obligations here."

"I'm coming down after this...this gentleman has his last toss." Laurel didn't dare look in the big blonde's direction. She didn't want him to become aware of her anxiety. "I was hoping we could have lunch together, Carter."

"I'm sorry, dear, but I enjoyed a pleasant meal with Mother and Aunt Polly about thirty minutes ago."

Oh, Lordy, Laurel thought, if Aunt Polly finds out about this, it'll be all over Tuscumbia before nightfall. She adored her slightly eccentric great-aunt, but the woman's penchant for gossip had often proven to be an embarrassment for Laurel. What was even worse was the old woman's tendency to blabbermouth family business to anyone willing to listen.

"That's all right. How about having a cola while I eat?" Laurel tried not to plead with Carter. She couldn't afford to let him know her real motive.

"I simply don't have time." Carter checked his fashionable Rolex. "I told you that being on the committee wouldn't leave me much time for you, Laurel dear. Anyway, you should lunch with Clintelle. She and Peter are very interested in placing weekly ads in the *Observer*."

"Hey, Miss Former Debutante," John said sternly, his voice revealing a jealousy he would never admit even to himself. "I'm ready anytime you are."

"Good Lord, Laurel, I can't understand how you could debase yourself this way, allowing that uncouth redneck to taunt you and then gape at your...your—"

"The man isn't a redneck, Carter. Can't you tell by his accent that he's a Yankee?" She had tried to pretend not to notice the man's voice. She didn't want to think about the fact that not only did he attract her in a way she abhorred, but he was, of all things, a Yankee.

"I don't have time to debate the issue with you." Carter brushed invisible lint off his crisp white slacks.

"Then go on," Laurel snapped in exasperation. "You'd better move before my Yankee dunks me again, and you get your clothes all wet."

Refusing to dignify Laurel's outburst with a reply, Carter Jackson Moody IV nonchalantly walked away, slipped behind the wheel of the "committee member" golf cart, and drove off, his perfectly groomed hair gleaming gun-metal silver, and not one drop of perspiration dotting his aristocratic brow.

"Her boyfriend's gone now, buddy," the friendly drunk called out. "Let's get on with the show. You got a bet to win."

Laurel tried to smile, but she couldn't. She was too mortified by the thought that she'd unconsciously referred to the stranger as her Yankee. Ever since she'd been a little girl and had first listened to Aunt Polly's tales of Pappy Drew being a dashing Union soldier who swept great-great-grandmother Clarice DuBois off her feet, Laurel had fantasized about a Yankee lover of her own.

She closed her eyes, silently praying to be spared from having to spend time with a man she feared could destroy the life she had planned for herself.

She opened her eyes and watched as the softball left his hand. It sailed smoothly into the target area, the strong, steady force of the throw hitting its mark. Laurel felt the seat give way beneath her. Then the water engulfed her once again. In the dark recesses of her mind, she wished she could stay under the surface, safe from facing what lay ahead.

With grit and determination, Laurel Drew surfaced quickly, like a bird taking flight. She was greeted by thunderous applause and earsplitting shouts and whistles. Dear God, what had she gotten herself into? She hated to admit that perhaps, just perhaps, Carter had been right all along. She was beginning to feel quite foolish. And if there was one thing on earth that she had no intention of ever being again, it was a fool.

"I'll take over now, Miss Drew," Jinn pulled off her T-shirt, threw it on the ground, and motioned for the older woman to exchange places with her. "You've got a lunch date with a Yankee hunk."

All the other girls' giggles rang in Laurel's ears as she slowly climbed down the narrow metal steps attached to the side of the tank.

"Have fun," Jinn said as she scrambled to the top of the tank.

Laurel reached for a dry towel, which lay across the back of a nearby lawn chair. She ran the cloth over her body, then began a vigorous massage of her long, black hair. She knew that her lunch date was watching her and that the Debutantes were watching him, but she refused to acknowledge either as she reached for her clothes.

John walked past the crowd and toward the booth while a dozen different men patted him on the back and congratulated him on his good fortune.

He stopped several feet away from his prize and watched as she tossed aside the damp towel and reached for a lavender flowered blouse. He'd never dreamed watching a woman dress could be so provocative. As his mermaid buttoned her blouse, pulled on a matching skirt, and slipped into white leather sandals, John's heart beat loud and fast, the sound of it roaring in his ears. His hands itched with the need to reach out and touch her. Damn! How could this woman arouse him by covering her body when it had been a long time since the sight of any other woman's naked body had done little more than vaguely interest him?

"Miss Drew." He walked over to her, offering his hand. "I'm John Mason, and I think we have a date."

"I'm Laurel Drew, and you're right, we do have an...an arrangement for lunch." Oh, he was big, she thought. Big and muscular and overpowering. He really wasn't any taller than Carter, but he was so much more... formidable.

Laurel Drew? he questioned. Hell, she couldn't be. Could she? Looking into the depths of her large, violet eyes, he decided that she very well could have written that hero-worshipping, romantic account of Johnny Drew.

"Hello, Laurel Drew." He didn't dare question her now. He could tell by her wary stance that she wasn't looking forward to paying the piper. She definitely didn't want to go anywhere with him. But why? God, she acted almost afraid of him. "Since I'm the stranger around here, you'll have to lead the way."

"Well...I...I don't know what to say, Mr. Mason. I assure you that I'm not in the habit of sharing a meal with a perfect stranger."

"Is that what I am, a perfect stranger?" He knew they'd met less than thirty minutes ago but was sure she felt the same twinge of familiarity that had plagued him since the first moment he'd seen her.

Laurel could not, would not, admit to this man that he evoked feelings of shared intimacies. No matter what her heart and body were saying, he was a stranger.

She tried to laugh, but it came out sounding more like a groan when John took her hand in his. "We've never met before."

"I wonder," he said softly.

"What?" Laurel stared into his searing brown eyes, eyes so dark they were almost black. She tugged on her hand, but he held it tightly.

"Strangers or not, I'm starving. How about taking me to some delicious food?"

"What would you like? There's an enormous variety. Everything from barbecue to pinto beans and corn bread."

"I'll let you decide." John removed his wallet from the back pocket of his tight-fitting jeans, pulled out a fifty-dollar bill, and handed it to Laurel.

She stood there speechless, gazing at the crisp green money in her hand. She didn't understand what was going on.

"For your little Debutantes," he said, grinning as his rough fingers stroked the top of her soft hand. "It was my part of the wager, remember?"

"But . . . but that was if you lost, which you didn't." She wished he'd stop rubbing her hand. Her stomach was doing flip-flops, and she didn't like the feeling one little bit.

"I'm always generous when I win."

Laurel handed the money to Jinn's "little sister" who seemed mesmerized by John Mason. "Here, Tara. Mr. Mason wants to make a donation."

"Food, woman, food!" John tugged on her arm, gently leading her away from the dunking booth.

"I'm coming, just don't drag me." She hoped her voice sounded harsh, but doubted if it had when he slowed his walk to a standstill and stood smiling at her. "I've been dying for a rosin-baked potato. They're across the road on the other side of the park."

"A what?" he asked.

"It's a potato sealed with pine resin and baked. They're delicious. I promise. I intend to splurge and get cheese."

"I doubt if a baked potato will fill me up." He held her hand securely in his, tightening his hold slightly when she tried to pull away.

"Will you please let go of my hand?"

"Why?"

"Why? Because . . . well, because it doesn't look right."

"It feels right," he said, deliberately rubbing the calloused inside of his hand against the softness of hers.

Laurel jerked on her hand. John held it securely for a fraction of a second, then released it. They stood there staring at each other. John took a deep breath, trying to control the desire to pick this woman up and fling her over his shoulder.

Laurel felt herself trembling. "Thank you." She forced herself to look away from his hard face. "Come on." She walked several steps away from him before he followed.

The farther they walked across the park, the more John became aware of the many peculiar looks coming their way. Undoubtedly a lot of people were wondering who was escorting Miss Laurel Drew.

Laurel sensed the curious stares coming from her friends and acquaintances. Clintelle Simpson watched them with open mouth and startled eyes. And Bonnie Jean Harland, with her arm around Carter's Uncle Wheeler, smiled and waved. Well, that was it, Laurel thought. I'm doomed. Bonnie Jean was sure to give her the third degree.

They made their way across the small park, which was centered around a pond formed by an underground spring. Ducks and swans swam peacefully across the mossy water's surface, occasionally waddling ashore to the delight of the children and adults who were feeding them.

A clear, blue, cloudless sky lay overhead, and John found himself squinting against the glare of the bright summer sun. The slight breeze was warm and humid, offering little relief from the stifling Southern heat. Dozens of booths and tents, crammed side by side, covered three-fourths of the area, while hordes of people milled around, looking, buying, eating, and listening. The sounds of hillbilly, bluegrass, and country music came from an open-air, rock-facade building towering two stories in the center of Spring Park.

The aroma of food mingled with the spicy smell of potpourri, scented candles, and dried-flower bouquets, as well as the pungent odor of human sweat. John's mouth felt dry, his skin damp, and his body hot and uncomfortable. He wasn't sure which was causing the last condition—the weather or his companion.

"This is it." Laurel stopped in front of a soft drink cart. "I'll get the colas, you get the potatoes right over there. And tell them I want the biggest one they've got, with plenty of cheese."

Within a few minutes, Laurel had led John across a newly constructed footbridge to an unoccupied grassy spot. She sat down and crossed her legs, Indian style, tucking her skirt beneath them. Setting her cola down beside her, Laurel tossed her head backward, letting her long hair caress her back as her face worshipped the sun.

John stared at the vision at his feet as the sunlight turned her hair blue-black and her lightly tanned skin to pure gold. He desperately wanted to touch her, to taste those full, pink lips. While his practical mind told him he was far too old and experienced to feel like a teenager in the throes of first love, his heart and body told him that they knew this woman, that she was his.

"Sit down, Mr. Mason. I can't pay off my bet if we don't share lunch."

John obeyed, joining her on the ground. "Call me John." He punched the plastic fork into the huge baked potato.

"All right," Laurel said, digging into her food. "Tell me, John, what are you doing in Tuscumbia? In the South for that matter? Don't tell me you came all the way from ... from ..."

"Ohio." The word was mumbled quickly after he swallowed a too-hot piece of potato.

"Ohio, huh? Did you come all the way from Ohio for the Keller Festival?"

He gulped down half his cup of cola trying to cool his throat. "As a matter of fact, I didn't. I'm on my way to Florida and stopped by here as a favor to my grandmother." He didn't want to lie to Laurel, but he was afraid that if he told her the entire truth immediately, she'd refuse to ever speak to him again. And for some insane reason, he wanted a chance to get to know this beautiful woman.

Laurel laughed, and the sound filled him with happiness. She certainly knew how to laugh. "Somehow, I can't picture you with a grandmother."

"Why is that?"

She couldn't tell him that he looked as if he'd sprung to life fully grown like some ancient demigod, filled with supernatural strength and potent virility. "Forget I said that. Tell me about your grandmother."

"Oh, she insisted I check into the possibility that her grandfather died in a Civil War skirmish around these parts. Since my grandfather's death last year, she's become a genealogy nut."

"Maybe I could help you. I'm an expert on the history of Colbert County. As a matter of fact, I'm a high school history teacher." What on earth had prompted her to offer this man assistance? He was dangerous. She knew that and still couldn't seem to free herself from the powerful attraction she felt for him.

"A history teacher?" For now, he'd have to pretend he didn't know anything about her. Later, much later, when he knew her better, he'd tell her the complete truth. "When I was in school, they didn't have teachers who looked like you."

"Oh, John, I've heard that one before. I think you could try to be more original."

"So, I'm not the first man to tell you how beautiful you are?" He knew damn well he wasn't. No doubt, Laurel had been told by hundreds of males that she was stunning.

She felt a warm flush spread across her cheeks and cursed her weakness. Yes, she knew she was beautiful. But her looks had always been a double-edged sword. Most men never cared to see beyond the surface to the intelligent woman beneath. Even the fact that she possessed a master's degree in history didn't convince the vast majority of people she met. "Thank you for the compliment, John."

Her icy reply alerted him to the fact that he had somehow hurt her feelings. Why should her looks be a sore spot with her? Most women would kill to be as beautiful as she was.

After her frigid comment, the two of them finished eating in silence, neither certain what to say or do next. Laurel finished the cola, then tilted the cup up to drop several pieces of ice into her mouth, and began to crunch.

"I knew it," John said, relieved to find something frivolous to talk about.

"Knew what?"

"I knew there had to be something about you that was unladylike."

"It's very ungentlemanly of you to say such a thing. Does my ice-crunching annoy you?" She knew it certainly annoyed Carter. He chided her endlessly about her bad habit.

"No, it doesn't annoy me in the least. As a matter of fact, I kind'a like it. It makes you seem very human." He wanted her to be human, a very human female, because she most definitely made him feel like a very human male. "I think there's something you should know about me."

"What's that?" No doubt there was a great deal she should know about him, but she knew she couldn't cope with this big man or his past life.

"I'm not a gentleman, Laurel. I'm an ex-lifer. I retired two weeks ago after twenty years in the Navy. I've got years of hard living behind me and an eagle tattooed on my arm."

"And a woman in every port?" She'd known all along what kind of man he was.

"Yeah, I probably did a long time ago when I was younger and my tastes weren't very discriminating." He wondered how they'd gotten around to talking about sex so fast. The last thing in the world he wanted to discuss with this Southern belle was the women in his past.

She didn't like the direction this conversation was taking. She could tell that he was uncomfortable talking about his sexual exploits. Compared to her one disastrous affair, his were probably so numerous he couldn't even remember half of them. "I...I really have to go. I'm due to work a shift at the Athletic Boosters booth, then the Friends of the Library booth, then—"

John reached out and covered her lips with his fingers. Immediately she stopped talking, her gaze locked defiantly with his. "I understand that your services are very much in demand, but I think you're running away."

Laurel's mouth moved beneath his fingertips, sending an unwanted current tingling through her body. She tried to speak but couldn't force the words into sound. They sat there on the hot, grassy earth, swarms of people walking around only a few yards away, and for one endless moment time stood still. Neither of them moved or spoke while their eyes exchanged dares and threats and promises.

Finally Laurel jerked free, pulling herself quickly to her feet. "I can't stay. I'll be late if I don't hurry."

"When can I see you again?" He couldn't let her leave without some kind of reassurance.

She stopped and stared at him, uncertainty wrinkling her brow. "John, I don't think it would be a good idea. Besides, I'm almost engaged," she lied.

"Really? Is that something like being almost pregnant?" Even though the tone of his words was teasing, he didn't smile.

Exasperated by his belligerent determination, Laurel planted her hands on her hips and glared at him. "Don't be absurd. It simply means that Carter Moody and I are...well...sort of have an understanding."

So, John wondered, does that mean she's sleeping with Pretty Boy? The thought made him want to hit something or somebody, preferably a tall, silver-haired Southern gentleman. "What about your promise to help me do a little historical research?"

"I didn't promise," Laurel said, wishing that she was anywhere on earth but here, arguing with a damned Yankee who was as different from her fantasy Yankee lover as a man could be. "I simply don't have the time to help you. I'm busy finishing my own research on a biography I'm writing about my great-great-grandfather." The moment the words were out, she regretted them. Her work on a lifelong dream was absolutely none of his business.

"It wouldn't take much of your time." Somehow he had to persuade her, and he knew using their one common interest might be his only hope. "I'll hang around here today until you're free to discuss it with me."

"I won't be free until late, and I have plans with Carter then." She didn't care that Carter might be too busy to share those plans. She simply couldn't allow herself to see John Mason again.

"I promise not to interfere with your plans. Just meet me for ten minutes. Please?"

"Oh, all right. Meet me back at the dunking booth around eight tonight, and I'll try to give you some pointers on how to find the information you want." A little voice within her warned that she would deeply regret agreeing to see him again.

John stood up and started walking toward her. Laurel stepped backward while she was still facing him. He took several large steps, moving his body directly in front of her. His thumb and forefinger gently gripped her chin. "Tonight." The word was a mere whisper.

Laurel's mouth trembled as she tried to smile and say goodbye. Instead, she merely nodded her head, turned quickly, and practically ran across the footbridge. John stood and watched until she disappeared into the crowd.

Two

Sunset painted the sky with burnished shades of red and orange and pink. Humid warmth still permeated the early evening air. Many craft booths and food vendors had closed their doors for the night, but huge crowds of people lingered in the park listening to the live band and waiting for the fireworks display.

John threw his half-smoked cigarette to the ground and crushed it with the heel of his shoe. He checked his watch. Ten till eight. He'd been standing by the dunking booth for five minutes wondering if he'd completely lost his mind. He hadn't been so eager to see a woman since he'd been twenty-one and madly in love with Cassie Whitson.

If he had any sense at all, he'd forget Laurel Drew, forget his promise to Gram, and head straight for St. Augustine. He'd been looking forward to seeing Nate again, spending a few weeks fishing, and sunning, and horsing around with his old Navy buddy. Admit it, he told himself, you've got the hots for this violet-eyed Southern belle.

Maybe it ran in the family. It could be in his genes. If ol' J. T. Andrews, Gram's grandfather, turned out to be Laurel's beloved ancestor, Johnny Drew, that would make them kissing cousins. He couldn't help but laugh at the thought. He knew Miss Former Debutante wouldn't find that fact amusing. From the newspaper article Gram had shown him, Laurel practically worshipped the memory of her paternal great-great-grandfather, as did the whole of Colbert County. For the life of him, he couldn't figure out how a former Yankee soldier became a local hero.

John felt her presence before he saw her standing a couple of yards away. He'd met a lot of women over the years but not one as beautiful as Laurel Drew. Obviously she hadn't had a chance to leave the park, because she still wore the same blouse and skirt she'd put on after her stint in the dunking booth. Her flawless complexion, devoid of make-up, glowed with a healthy tan.

John couldn't remember when he'd ever spent so much time looking at a woman's face. But then, he'd never seen eyes the color of Gram's African violets, or such full pink lips. Lips that he longed to feel exploring his body.

His dark eyes traveled the length of her form, taking special note of her generous breasts and tiny waist. No doubt his hands could easily span her waistline, but she wasn't a small woman, definitely not petite, not even fashionably slender. He guessed she was about five-foot-five, and every ounce of her was rounded into delectable curves.

Where her hair had appeared blue-black in the noontime sun, it looked like ebony silk in the twilight. A few stray tendrils fell across her forehead, the rest hung in luxurious waves to her shoulders.

John took several steps toward her, hesitating when she moved forward. She smiled, and he felt an unwanted warmth spread through his lower body. Somehow he'd just have to find a way to get Laurel into his bed.

Every instinct within Laurel raged with warnings. John Mason wasn't a man who played by the rules she lived by. He'd told her himself that he wasn't a gentleman. So why am I here? she wondered. She knew she could use her argument with Carter as an excuse. After all, she'd planned such a lovely, romantic evening for them. She had every right to be upset that he wanted them to share their time with several other couples. Couples who had been his friends when he'd been married. It wasn't that she'd ever been jealous of Carter's deceased wife, Kathie Lou. She'd known the woman and liked her. She simply wanted time alone with the man who seemed destined to become her husband.

Laurel took a few more steps, stopping less than two feet away from John. In the soft light of sunset, his hair seemed darker. Cut short and carelessly styled, it beckoned her fingers to reach out and touch. He stared at her, his deep-set eyes saying things she didn't want to hear, sending a message as old as time. His heavy brows and thick lashes were an earthy brown, as was the thick whorl of chest hair exposed by the open buttons of his well-fitting shirt.

Unbidden, the thought of his naked chest flashed through her mind. I do not want to see him without his shirt, she told herself. She'd simply talk to him for a while, perhaps even deliberately maneuver him over to where Carter could see them walk by. She'd spend twenty or thirty minutes with him, explain all the procedures to take in tracing a Civil War ancestor, shake his hand, and say goodbye.

She didn't have room in her life for a man like John Mason. Someday she'd probably marry Carter and have a couple of children. Children who could trace their bloodlines on both sides of the family back to the founding fathers of Alabama, of the United States, even as far back as the shores of Europe. But this summer she was going to complete her biography of Pappy Drew. The University Press was eagerly awaiting the manuscript. Nothing and no one was going to stand between her and this lifelong dream.

Most definitely not some Northerner who bore no resemblance in looks or nature to Grandmother Clarice's dashing Yankee lover.

John moved to stand directly in front of her. He looked down into her eyes and smiled. She opened her mouth to speak but couldn't. Her breath caught in her throat. A sensation of exhilaration and fear hit the pit of her stomach. It was like nothing she'd ever felt in her whole life.

"Hi." He looked at her for a few minutes then reached out to take her hand.

"H...ah...hello." She jerked her hand away, the feel of his flesh against hers burning her like fire.

John eyed her quizzically. "Thanks for meeting me."

"I can't stay long," she said, clasping her hands in front of her, nervously rubbing them together.

"I'll take whatever I can get."

Telling herself that he hadn't meant his remark to sound suggestive, Laurel smiled pleasantly, trying to project an aura of self-confidence she most certainly didn't feel. "Do you want to walk around while we talk, or would you prefer to find a place to sit down?"

"We could walk for a while, then find something to eat, and find a place to sit and watch the fireworks." He knew she'd said she couldn't stay long, but the very fact that she seemed reluctant made him all the more determined to keep her at his side for as long as he could. There probably wasn't a snowball's chance in hell she'd end up in his bed tonight. Instinctively he felt she wasn't the type for one-night stands. But neither was he, really. Not in years. Not since he'd grown older, more discriminating.

"We'll walk, but I don't have time for anything to eat." She tried very hard not to keep staring at him but couldn't help herself. He wasn't handsome, but he was sexy, the sexiest man she'd ever met. She wondered if he had this effect on all women or just her. Then she remembered the long-legged blonde at the dunking booth today, and her whole body tensed with feelings of anger and...jealousy? No, not jealousy. How could she feel jealousy over a man she barely knew?

John reached out and took her small hand into his large one. The feel of his work-roughened palm against her smooth one shot electrically charged sensations up her arm and into her bloodstream.

"Let's walk down toward the spring," he said, taking a step. When she didn't move, he tugged on her hand. "While I was looking around today, I thought I saw a secluded spot with trees and benches."

Laurel pulled her hand out of his. "There are no secluded spots in Spring Park during the festival."

John took her hand again. When she glared up at him, he smiled and squeezed her fingers gently. Laurel glanced around quickly, wondering how this would look to her acquaintances. They had seen her once today with this big, blond Yankee. What would they think if they saw her holding hands with him?

Laurel fell into step beside John, her hand lightly gripping his. As they walked, he maneuvered his body closer and closer to hers until her shoulder touched the side of his arm. She knew she had to find a way to disengage her hand without making a scene, but she wasn't quite sure how to go about it.

"Are you telling me that all the young lovers have no hope of finding any privacy around here?" He noticed that she wasn't looking at him but straight ahead. And she kept trying to put some distance between their bodies. Undoubtedly he wasn't the only one getting aroused by just holding hands.

"Maybe you should tell me exactly what you know about this ancestor of yours, and then I'll know if I can help you." Laurel wished John would allow her to put a few inches between them. Every time she moved away, he followed, his arm pressing her bare shoulder, his hand, clasped around her, brushing with feather-light strokes against her leg.

"All I know is what my grandmother has told me." John felt a quivering sensation in Laurel's body when he allowed his hand to linger at the side of her leg, his knuckles pressing gently into her thigh. "It seems her grandfather, J.T. Andrews, left his young bride and went off to fight in the war. He joined the Ohio Ninth as a lieutenant. His father, being a man of wealth and influence, made sure his son didn't enter as a private."

Laurel pulled lightly on her hand and eased it out of John's. She remained close to his side as they continued to walk. "There was a great deal of that on both sides," she laughed as she turned her head to catch a glimpse of John's rugged face. She wondered when he'd shaved last. He had a five o'clock shadow. Obviously his beard, like his chest hair, was much darker than the spun gold covering his head.

"Sometime in the spring of 1862, his father received a letter saying that J.T. had been badly wounded, supposedly killed at Shiloh. Several weeks later, the family received a second letter from General Mitchell, a friend of J.T.'s father. The General said that J.T. had died in Tuscumbia and had been buried there."

"How strange." Laurel was well acquainted with all of Tuscumbia's Civil War history, and she'd never heard of this Lieutenant Andrews.

"Yeah, I know. But Gram wanted me to check it out. Since my grandfather died, this Genealogical Society she joined has become one of her reasons for living."

"Has she thought to contact the National Archives and Records Service in Washington?" Laurel asked.

"She got some information there and some from the state archives. According to those records, John Terrence Andrews was listed as missing in action, presumed dead at Shiloh. That information and the letter from this General Mitchell don't coincide."

"That is odd. Has your grandmother had someone check the *OR?*"

"The what?"

"Oh, I'm sorry. I forget that everyone isn't as familiar with historical research as I am. The *OR* is a 128-volume set of *Official Records of the Union and Confederate Armies in the War of Rebellion.*"

John smiled. "It's nice to meet an intelligent woman. No wonder you're thinking about writing a book."

Warmth filled Laurel's body. A strange sense of awareness spread through her like life-giving rain covering parched earth. She'd only met this man today, and yet he'd already seen past her looks to the mind inside, to the part of her few men cared to know about. "Thank you."

She hadn't realized she'd acknowledged his compliment until he spoke. "Thanks for what?"

Laurel laughed, trying to conceal her embarrassment. "Just thanks for realizing that there's more to me than... than..."

"Than a beautiful face and a gorgeous body?" He saw the vulnerable look in her eyes and wondered who had put it there. John felt a momentary twinge of conscience. She had thanked him for a compliment that he hadn't even been aware he was giving.

"Yes. I can't believe you understand. We don't even know each other." There it was again, she thought, that feeling of familiarity.

"Hey, in all honesty, I have to admit that it wasn't exactly your brain that first attracted me to you today."

"No?" Her smile widened, her eyes brightened. "Then what was it?"

Picking up on her joking manner, he responded, "It was your eyes. I'd never seen purple eyes before."

Laurel burst into laughter. "I don't... have," she giggled, "purple eyes."

"Violet, blue-violet." He watched her face lift toward his like a flower to the sun. Those huge cat eyes should have been green or gold, but they weren't. They were deep and dark, a shade lighter than blue-black grapes.

Laurel's breath caught in her throat when he tugged on her hand pulling her forward. Her breasts pushed against his hard chest. "You're the first man . . . who ever said my eyes were . . . the first thing that attracted him."

"Oh, what do they usually say is the first thing?" He watched her lips part and thought he'd die if he didn't kiss her.

Laurel stared up at him, mesmerized by the look of raw hunger in his brown eyes. She felt herself drawn to him, found herself drowning in the dark depths of his gaze, and knew if she didn't pull away from him he would kiss her. A war raged within her heart and mind. Reason won over emotions. Laurel closed her eyes, blotting out the sight of his passion, and tried to draw away from him. John released her hands the moment he felt her resistance.

Their bodies no longer touching, John and Laurel looked at each other as a hot breeze stroked them, the loud beat of a "She-done-him-wrong" song caressed them, and the smell of their own male-female essence assailed them.

"I've got to go," Laurel said quickly, needing to put some distance between them. She felt like a small, trapped animal. The need to escape overwhelmed her.

"Are you meeting your boyfriend?" John hadn't meant for the words to sound so harsh, but the thought of her with another man tore at his insides. He knew he shouldn't care. She was nothing to him. Just another woman. A beautiful, sexy, intriguing woman.

"I . . . uh . . ." She had no intention of meeting Carter but knew she shouldn't admit the truth to this man. "No, no, I'm not. He's busy entertaining some friends."

"Then stay with me."

"I'm sorry. I can't." She took several steps backward.

"Hey, no," he said, his hand reaching out for her, an expression of pain crossing his rough-hewn face. "I need some more information about ol' J.T." At this precise moment, he didn't give two hoots about ol' J.T., but he was willing to use any trick in the book to keep her with him a while longer.

"I . . ." she wanted to say "I can't," but the words in her mind wouldn't take form on her tongue. Fool, she chided herself. Fool. "Okay. Buy me a funnel cake, and we'll find a place to sit and talk."

"Buy you a what?"

"A funnel cake," she laughed, nodding her head in the direction of the food booths behind them. "Oh, you know. They're swirly fried batter covered with sugar and cinnamon."

"Should I just follow my nose?" Leaning back his head, John drew in a deep breath. A hundred different aromas blended together, some distinct odors overpowering subtler ones.

"Forget that, just follow me." Laurel was tempted to reach out and take his hand while she led him to the food vendors. It was a temptation she forced herself to overcome. "Now smell. I love cinnamon. Aunt Polly makes the most delicious French toast smothered in cinnamon."

They joined a long line of people waiting their turn to purchase the sweet treat. As others came in behind them, John moved closer and closer to Laurel, finally easing himself directly behind her. He placed one hand at her waist and pulled her back against him. The moment their bodies touched, he knew he'd made a mistake, but he couldn't move, and he didn't want her to. When the line began moving forward, he eased his arm around her waist and moved to stand beside her.

Neither of them talked. Neither of them knew what to say. Finally reaching the counter, John ordered two funnel cakes and was amazed by the sight of the large concoctions covering the surface of white paper plates. Cinnamon filled his nostrils, and he knew that after today the fragrance of this particular spice would always remind him of this special woman.

Laurel brought the plate up to her mouth, her tongue licking across the top to taste the scrumptious confection. "I have a weakness for sweets." Oh, what a stupid thing to say, she thought. After nearly ten minutes of complete silence, why did she have to make such a silly confession?

"What else do you have a weakness for, Laurel Drew?"

Ignoring his question, Laurel walked steadily toward the spring. She hesitated briefly from time to time to speak and reply when spoken to. Without question, John followed her through the crowd, over a bridge, and across the road.

"It'll be less crowded on the hillside here until it's time for the fireworks."

John gazed up at the grass-covered hill. Two paved streets going into the town flanked each side of the area. He noticed several couples, a few with small children, scattered about on the hill.

"I wish I'd thought to get a blanket out of the car. Sitting on this grass could get itchy." She looked around. Locating what she thought was the perfect spot, Laurel sat down, stretched out her legs in front of her, and patted the ground beside her. "Won't you join me?"

"Anytime, any place," John replied as he sat down and stretched out his long legs. He looked at their limbs lying side by side in the grass. He wanted to reach out and run his hand up the smooth tanned beauty of her calves, caress the full firmness of her thighs, explore the softness of her... He had to stop thinking about touching her. This woman was a lady. He had nothing to offer her, nothing she'd want.

"The fireworks will start as soon as it's dark." Laurel bit into her cake. She turned to catch John staring at her. "Eat. Eat. It's better when it's still hot."

Obeying, John bit into the dessert. It was warm and sweet and spicy. He decided that funnel cakes and Laurel Drew had something in common. He suddenly longed for the taste of woman instead of the taste of sugar.

"Well, what do you think? Good, huh?"

"Delicious." He looked at her mouth.

Laurel willed herself not to blush. She was far too mature to let the flirtations of this hot-blooded Yankee get under her skin. "I hope you won't be disappointed by the fireworks display. You've probably been all over the world and seen some spectacular shows. Ours only lasts about fifteen minutes, but for that one-quarter of an hour it lights up the sky."

"I won't be disappointed."

"How can you be so sure?"

"It's who you share the event with and not the event itself that makes something special."

For just a split second, Laurel couldn't breathe. How could some roughneck Yankee sailor say something so beautiful? Maybe he wasn't quite as uncouth as she'd thought. "So, tell me about your life in the Navy."

John swallowed a mouthful of cake. "That's a tall order. But here goes. I joined at eighteen as an act of defiance against my grandfather. He wanted me to go to college. I wanted to get away from him. When I was twenty-one, I decided to test for Officer's Training School. I passed the tests but changed my mind and stayed an enlisted man. I've been everywhere and done everything." He laughed when he saw the look of shock in her eyes turn to suspicion and then humor.

"What about the tattoo and the girl in every port?"

"I'll show you the tattoo one of these days when I have a reason to take off my shirt." He watched her eyes lower to his chest, her hot gaze almost singeing him with its intensity. "As for the girl in every port—"

"Have you ever been married?" She could have bitten off her tongue. Damn, why had she asked him that? He'd think she was interested.

When he didn't immediately reply, Laurel wondered if she'd accidentally hit a sore spot. What would she say if he asked her about her love life? What would she tell him about Carter? More important, what would she tell him about her past?

"I was married once a long time ago. It was a big mistake on both our parts. I haven't seen Cassie in fifteen years." He seldom thought about the girl he'd married or how their brief marriage had ended. She was a part of his life he'd rather forget, one of the most painful parts.

"Nothing serious in fifteen years?"

"Nope. What about you and this Carter? Why aren't you already married?"

"Carter and I have know each other all our lives. Our families are good friends."

"So?" He saw a tiny sprinkling of powdered sugar in the corner of her mouth. He wanted to remove it with his tongue.

"Carter's nearly twelve years older than I am. He's a widower. We've only been dating about a year. Neither of us wants to rush into anything." She knew that wasn't exactly the truth. Marriage was something she and Carter had never discussed, even though the whole town seemed to think they were the ideal couple. The strongest emotion she'd ever felt for Carter was sisterly affection. But she most certainly wasn't going to tell John Mason that her heart wasn't committed to another man. Carter might prove to be the only protection she had against her own stupidity.

John looked at her mouth while she nibbled on the funnel cake. When she licked the sugar from her lips, he groaned silently. He figured if she'd been dating Pretty Boy for over a year, then they'd made love. Right now he didn't want to talk about Carter or any other men in her life.

"What did you do in the Navy?" She decided it was best if they didn't get too involved in conversation about their love lives. Keep it light, keep it casual, she told herself. Maybe you can handle these unwanted yearnings if you can steer clear of too many personal revelations.

"I was a Chief Petty Officer. I spent the last four years in San Diego training recruits."

"It sounds like we have something in common."

He stared at her, a puzzled look on his face.

"You trained recruits, I teach teenagers."

John found the comparison amusing but had to admit she was partially right. "Yeah, but from what I understand about schools these days, I probably had the easier job."

They laughed together, sharing feelings of intense familiarity and budding desire.

"Why did you retire?" Laurel leaned back on her elbows, her long hair touching the grass.

"Several different reasons. I've got a friend who retired last year who wants me to go into business with him in St. Augustine. Then I've got a grandmother who wants me to come home to Sterling, Ohio, get married and give her some great-grandchildren. Somehow I wanted to make a change in my life. I just haven't decided what that change is going to be on a permanent basis."

"I suppose it's hard to make a decision when life is pulling you in different directions."

"What about you, Laurel? Do you know what you want out of life?" Damn, he wished she'd lick off that last smidgen of sugar from her mouth. If she didn't, he was going to do it for her.

"Ever since I was about ten, I've wanted to write Pappy Drew's biography. Finally that dream is about to come true. I have to finish the book this summer and have it on the editor's desk by September first."

John could see the passion, the enthusiasm in her violet eyes. God, he felt terrible about keeping the truth from her.

Maybe he should tell her. At least he could suggest the possibility that Johnny Drew might have been both a deserter and a bigamist. "Writing this book means a lot to you, doesn't it?"

"Oh, John, you can't imagine how much. Johnny Drew is practically a legend in these parts. He was a man who gave up everything—his family, his country—for the woman he loved." Laurel could hear Aunt Polly's voice weaving the spell of enchanted love, the story that had mesmerized Laurel from the age of four.

"How did a Yankee become so revered in the heart of Dixie?"

"He was wounded at Shiloh and was recovering when his regiment came through this area. When some of his own soldiers accosted grandmother Clarice, Johnny defended her. Unfortunately there was a scuffle, Johnny's wounds reopened, his fellow soldiers ran off, and there Clarice was left with the enemy. She had him taken to her home and nursed him back to health. During that time, they fell in love."

"Why should falling in love with an Alabama girl make him a legend?"

"Nobody knows the exact details, but Clarice's father reported to Johnny's commanding officer that Johnny had died. How they pulled that off is a mystery. But we do know that he worked, sort of undercover, for the Confederacy after that."

"The man was a traitor?" John wondered if perhaps Laurel already knew what kind of man old J.T. Andrews had been.

"He most certainly was not! Well, not if you think of him as a Confederate."

"What did this Johnny Drew do after the war ended?"

"He worked with and for the people of North Alabama. He and Carter's great-grandfather were owners and publishers of the *Observer*. Carter still owns the weekly newspaper today. Pappy Drew was so well liked and respected, he was elected to the state Senate for four terms. He was strong, intelligent, brave, and wildly in love with his wife.'' With a fiery exhilaration burning in her eyes, Laurel reached out and grasped John's arm as if beseeching him to see the man who lived so vividly in her heart and mind.

How can I destroy this fantasy she's deluding herself with? he wondered. How do I even broach the subject? ''For a man to give up everything, he must have been very much in love.''

''He was,'' Laurel sighed, and her eyes locked with John's. All her life Laurel had longed for a man to love her the way Johnny Drew had loved Clarice DuBois. A strong, fearless man willing to love against all the odds. A man who would capture her heart and claim her body. Laurel closed her eyes, fighting the sensations coursing through her. Her hand on John's arm began to tremble, yet she couldn't break the contact of his flesh against her own. All her life she'd wanted what her great-great-grandmother had shared with one special man.

''Laurel?'' John's deep voice softened to a whisper, her name representing a hundred questions soaring through his mind. He didn't want this wild feeling consuming him. He didn't need a woman like Laurel Drew in his life. He didn't want any complications, but he sure as hell wanted this violet-eyed sorceress. He wanted her like he'd never wanted a woman before, not even Cassie. And he'd loved Cassie.

Laurel opened her eyes and tried to focus on John's rugged face, but a fine sheen of tears blurred her vision. She told herself that this man was not her fantasized Yankee lover. He wasn't dashing or charming or wildly in love with her. He was a rough, crude ex-sailor out for a good time. She jerked her arm away. She eased her body down onto the ground, her back against the soft grass, her eyes staring up into the night sky.

''Laurel, I—''

"Shh. Don't say anything."

John lay down beside her, propping himself up with one arm. He bent over her, uncaring that dozens of people were scattered over the hill, that darkness barely concealed their identities.

Laurel looked up into his black eyes. His jaw was clenched, his nostrils flared. She realized that he was struggling with his emotions just as she was. He doesn't want this anymore than I do, she thought. But he can't help himself. And neither can I.

She saw his hand moving toward her face. His index finger traced around the edges of her full mouth, stopping in the corner, moving in a circular motion. John pulled his hand away from her face and licked his finger, the finger that had caressed her lips.

"Sugar," he said in a hoarse whisper.

"Wh...what?" Laurel forced herself to breathe. She felt as if her chest had suddenly filled with too much air, and she was smothering.

"You had sugar in the corner of your mouth."

"Oh."

"I wanted to lick it away, but . . ."

She moaned softly, the pain in her body taking verbal form.

In the soft, summer darkness, John Mason lowered his head, and with great restraint, touched his lips to Laurel Drew's. He groaned. She sighed. And the night sky exploded with fireworks. At the thundering, popping sound, Laurel's body jerked, but her lips still clung to John's.

The sky above Spring Park filled with a thousand sparkling, gleaming shards of multicolored lights. Laurel reached up and touched the side of John's face, her warm fingers stroking the stubble covering his jaw. He moaned once. Then his mouth took hers. Wild and hot and sweet, their lips and tongues mated.

He wanted more. She wanted more. And for one torrid moment their only thoughts were of joining their bodies in life's most intimate embrace. But the sound of adult voices mingling with children's laughter intruded on their private interlude. John slowed the kiss gradually, allowing them both to gain some control. Finally he rested his forehead against hers, his breathing harsh and labored as if he'd just run several miles.

"Laurel, are you all right?"

She pushed him away and sat up. She couldn't bring herself to look at him. She'd never known such intense feelings. It frightened her to think that she could lose control as she had. And in Spring Park with hordes of people all around. What if someone had seen her? What would Carter think if he knew? Or Aunt Polly? Or heaven forbid, her mother. Gertrude Drew had raised her daughter to be a lady. And a lady would never succumb to the feelings that were still raging within Laurel.

"Honey, it's all right," John said. "You didn't do anything to be ashamed of."

She knew she had to get away from this man, from this big Yankee with his mesmerizing black eyes and persuasive mouth. When she got up, John immediately did the same, but when he reached out for her, she quickly stepped away. "I've got to go."

"No." He knew that he'd frightened her with his aggressive behavior, but dammit, she'd wanted that kiss just as much as he had.

"Please, John, let me go."

"When will I see you again?"

"I...I..." She didn't dare see him again. He was dangerous. He wasn't the kind of man she wanted or needed in her life.

"Tomorrow? Spend the day with me tomorrow?" He couldn't remember ever wanting anything so much.

"No. I can't."

"Please."

"No...I...I'm the hostess at the DuBois-Drew Home tomorrow." Her voice trembled when she spoke. "Our house is on the tour of homes. I have to be there to guide the tourists and tell them about the house, about my family."

"About Johnny Drew?"

"Yes." She took several steps away from him. "I have to go."

"Good night, Mermaid." He had to let her go for now, but tomorrow was another day, and right or wrong, wise or foolish, he had every intention of seeing Laurel Drew again.

Three

———

John pulled his red convertible up beside the last car parked in a row of tourists' vehicles outside the DuBois-Drew Home. Although his ticket was for the complete tour, John was interested in only one house. The house where Laurel Drew was playing hostess for the day.

He'd spent a long, restless night thinking about the woman, recalling every feature of her beautiful face, every curve of her soft body. The kiss they'd shared had been the sweetest thing John had ever experienced. Never had he been aroused by something so innocent. If they ever made love, the whole world was likely to explode.

He sat there in his new Jaguar XJ-S, the sleek, much-adored mustering-out gift he'd given himself. He'd managed to save quite a bit of money while he'd been in the Navy, and a few shrewd investments he'd made with his old buddy Nate kept his bank account in the black. But he knew money wouldn't impress a woman like Laurel. She'd be impressed with pretty speeches and gentlemanly manners, and a lineage he could trace back to the Revolutionary War.

John wondered what kind of reception he'd receive from the lovely Miss Drew. She probably hoped she'd never see his ugly face again. He knew she didn't want to be attracted to him, knew she'd fight against any kind of involvement. They were different kinds of people, from different worlds. Even though their minds were well aware of the fact, he guessed their bodies didn't know the difference and wouldn't care if they did.

If possible, it was hotter today than yesterday. The blazing afternoon sun warmed John's face as he leaned his head back against the leather seat.

A steady traffic of tourists went in and out of the mansion, some remaining to tour the grounds, others snapping pictures, while a few drove away heading for the next historical home. John sat in his car for quite a while, watching, waiting, and building up his courage. It had been a long time since he'd let his desire for a woman overrule his good sense.

He opened the car door and got out, standing braced against the front fender as he took a long, hard look at the famous DuBois-Drew Home. He'd never seen anything like it outside of an old movie, he thought. *Gone With the Wind* maybe. His grandparents' home in Ohio was a fine old house, built in the late twenties, but compared to this place, Dora Jansen's home wasn't much more than a hovel. He'd known all along that Laurel was out of his league. Even if she wasn't rich, she was saturated with the kind of breeding that took generations to acquire. She was a real lady, and he was no gentleman.

Rubbing his jaw, John pulled away from the car and walked slowly behind a small group of twittering old ladies.

"I can hardly wait to see inside this place," one lavender-haired senior citizen remarked. "You know that Clarice DuBois nursed her Yankee lover back to health in the attic of this old home, and when the war ended, she married him in the front parlor.''

"Indeed," her plump companion said. "I read the great-great-granddaughter's article in the *Observer*. That's why Maudie and I came all the way from Birmingham for this festival."

John wondered how many other people had been drawn to the Keller Festival by Laurel's article in her boyfriend's weekly newspaper. Women were always fascinated by a love story, even one over a century old. Perhaps it was the forbidden aura that surrounded a Southern belle capturing the heart of a Union soldier. He could just imagine what these little old ladies would say if he told them the dashing Johnny Drew had left behind a pregnant young bride in Ohio when he'd wooed and won the lovely Clarice.

John hesitated for a few minutes, allowing the chattering group ahead of him to enter the front portico. He watched as two young girls in enormous hoopskirts greeted the visitors and escorted them to the front door.

John didn't know much about architecture and even less about old Southern mansions, but even with his limited knowledge, he knew enough to be impressed with Laurel's home. From where he stood, he could see the huge white columns extended across the front and both sides of the house. Sixteen columns!

When John stepped onto the veranda, one of the costumed girls smiled and spoke. "Good afternoon, sir, and welcome to the DuBois-Drew Home, which was built during 1834 to 1836 by workers brought from Etienne Dubois's plantation near New Orleans."

The other young lady opened the door as the first took John's arm and escorted him into the foyer. A small, fine-boned woman in her seventies approached them, a smile of welcome softening the delicately lined face.

"Hello. I'm Polly Drew. I'm afraid my niece has already started the tour. Would you like to join them or wait until the next one?"

"I'll . . . I'll join this one if it's all right."

"Certainly. Follow me. Laurel always starts with the gentlemen's parlor."

Polly Drew led John a few yards down the foyer to where the group of elderly ladies gazed appreciatively while Laurel Drew described the room before them.

When Laurel paused for a moment, her aunt tugged on John's arm and led him forward. "Oh, Laurel, dear, we have a late arrival. Could you possibly reiterate the highlights of your little speech?"

Laurel turned, a warm smile on her pink lips. Her eyes met John's and she froze, the smile fading quickly. John wasn't sure what she was thinking. Obviously she was shocked to see him, but was it a pleasant or unpleasant surprise?

Everyone in the foyer stopped talking as they looked back and forth from the big blond man to their elegant guide dressed in Clarice Dubois's pink and silver ball gown. Neither John nor Laurel was aware that they had become the center of attention. Only Aunt Polly's discreet nudge in Laurel's ribs brought the scene to an end.

"Uh . . . uh . . . yes, the dress. The dress I'm wearing belonged to my great-great-grandmother, Laurel Clarice DuBois Drew. It was made in Paris, purchased by Clarice's father, Etienne DuBois, and given to her to wear for her eighteenth birthday, which was celebrated by a ball given in this very house."

Laurel wished that John Mason wouldn't look at her with those passion-filled black eyes. She was well aware of the fact that her full breasts swelled seductively above the bodice of her satin gown, and that John's gaze rested exactly there. She could feel her breasts tightening, her nipples hardening under his heated gaze. Her own body was betraying her, and there was nothing she could do about it.

John was certain his presence disturbed her, and he was glad because her presence sure as hell was disturbing him. He imagined that ol' J.T. had been as aroused by the sight of Clarice in that dress as he was by Laurel. No wonder the man had deserted the army and committed bigamy. He'd be tempted to do the same for Laurel. Shaking his head, John tried to force himself to think clearly..

He stared at the room open before them. Obviously they'd moved on from the gentlemen's parlor while he'd been daydreaming.

"And this is the ladies' parlor," Laurel said. "Please take note of the superbly carved Carrara marble mantel, which is enriched by the hand-carved rosewood trimming of the John Belter sofa."

John followed from room to room, watching Laurel's every move and occasionally hearing parts of her speech. As the minutes ticked by, John and Laurel both grew more and more tense. By the time they descended the spiral staircase in the entrance hall, Laurel's hands were trembling, and John was trying to stay a discreet distance behind the group in the hopes none of them would notice his arousal. John cursed his lack of control.

"Now," Laurel said, smiling pleasantly, purposely not looking in John's direction, "if you'll follow me to the back veranda, Aunt Polly has some deliciously cool lemonade for y'all."

The soft swish of satin against stiff crinoline called attention to Laurel's movement as she turned, leading the tourists down the hallway to the outside. When he stopped and waited for the crowd to disappear, John felt relieved to have a few minutes alone. He needed time to pull himself together, and if he had any sense at all, march right out the front door, get in his car, and drive hard and fast to St. Augustine. He didn't need the complication of Laurel Drew in his life right now. He had enough problems without becoming obsessed with a woman who could offer him nothing but misery.

He turned and took a few tentative steps toward the front door. He decided the only sensible thing to do was run, to get away from Laurel before it was too late. He'd call Gram from Nate's once he got to Florida. He'd tell her... what? This wild-goose chase she'd sent him on was just one of her whims. It couldn't possibly matter to her what had happened to ol' J.T.

Think Florida, he told himself. Sun, beaches, half-naked women. Fishing and boating and raising hell with Nate. He had a chance for a new life, a second chance at being a civilian. He and Nate were two of a kind, a couple of old swabbies with commitments to no one but themselves. Why didn't the thought of sun and fun with a variety of bathing beauties give him enough incentive to walk out the door and leave Southern hospitality behind?

"My goodness," Aunt Polly said as she sashayed up behind John and placed a frail hand on his arm. "Surely you aren't leaving without tasting some of my lemonade?"

Startled by the woman's unexpected appearance, John tensed momentarily before turning to greet Laurel's aunt. "Uh, why, no. Of course not, Mrs. Drew. Please, lead the way to the refreshments."

Polly placed her arm through John's, and together they joined the others on the back veranda where several tourists had seated themselves on white wicker chairs and settees.

"How many acres surround this plantation house?" one of the tourists asked.

"Presently there are only seventy acres. Originally there were over four hundred," Laurel replied. "We've tried to preserve the grounds, to keep the gardens as close to their original design as possible."

"Oh, my dear, we're all so eager for the biography of your great-great-grandfather to be published. Your aunt told us that the University Press will be putting it out sometime next year," Maudie said.

"It must be a romance," another said. "After all, with a title like *Yankee Lover* what else could it be?"

Laurel stiffened when she saw her aunt offering John Mason a glass of lemonade. She had hoped he'd left. No, she'd more than hoped, she'd actually prayed. Her life was already planned. The last thing on earth she needed was some sexy heartbreaker leading her astray. She had ignored her family's and friends' warnings about an uncouth scoundrel far beneath her socially. In college, she'd been fascinated by Scott Baker, a man so unlike her father and uncles, her cousins and former boyfriends. Once she'd stepped down from the pedestal where all the Drew women had been placed. But never again!

Think about your book, she reminded herself. Think about fulfilling a lifelong dream. Think about Carter and the kind of life you can have as his wife. They shared generations of family tradition and honor, which they could proudly pass down to their children and grandchildren. She mustn't allow desire for a stranger to interfere with her plans. Laurel couldn't help remembering that Clarice DuBois had taken a chance by giving her heart and body to an enemy soldier, and that their love had conquered all. But Laurel wasn't her great-great-grandmother, and John Mason could never become her Yankee lover.

"The biography? Yes...the biography of Johnny Drew does center around his love for Clarice DuBois, a love so great that he gave up everything he held dear." Unable to stop herself, Laurel glanced at the big man leisurely drinking lemonade, his huge hand completely covering the small paper container. He was looking directly at her, his eyes touching her cheek, caressing her neck, kissing her parted lips. No. Eyes can't caress. Eyes can't kiss. But she knew that John's could and had. She felt warmly aroused as if his hands and lips had actually made contact with her body.

"I...uh... Please feel free to tour the grounds before you leave." Laurel desperately wanted to put some distance between her and the man whose very look held danger.

"I'm sorry to interrupt, Laurel, but we have another group waiting in the entrance hall," Aunt Polly said as she lifted the hem of her long dress, stepped around John, and waved a thank you to the young front-door hostess who had whispered the news to her from the back doorway.

When the crowd moved off the veranda toward the beautiful rose garden in the rear, Laurel took a deep breath and faced her aunt and John.

"Hello," he said, but didn't make a move toward or away from her.

"Hello, Joh...Mr. Mason." Laurel turned to her aunt and tried to smile a nothing's-wrong-with-me smile. "Aunt Polly, this is John Mason, a...a visitor from Ohio. Mr. Mason, my aunt, Mrs. Polly Hallmark Drew."

Before John could respectfully acknowledge the introduction, Polly gasped, "You're a Yankee, Mr. Mason. How delightful. My goodness, Laurel, wherever did you find this young rogue?"

Laurel's face reddened an unbecoming shade as her eyes flashed up to John's face. She could tell that he found the situation amusing. "Uh..." Laurel cleared her throat. "Perhaps you could show Mr. Mason the grounds before he leaves."

"Why don't you show him the grounds, dear? I could give the next tour." A glint of mischief glowed in the elderly Mrs. Drew's pale gray eyes. "I know this young man would enjoy hearing more about Southern belles and dashing Yankees."

Some inner demon urged Laurel to agree to her aunt's outrageous suggestion. She wanted to show John the DuBois-Drew plantation. She wanted to walk alone with him in the gardens, to take him for a stroll in the privacy of the woods, to stand in the shade of centuries-old trees and whisper his name.

"I have to go." Ignoring her aunt's startled expression and John's mocking chuckle, Laurel rushed inside the house.

Polly Drew nodded her head affirmatively as if she'd just realized some great truth, then turned to the man who stood beside her staring at the open back door. "Well, Mr. Mason, why don't we sit down and have a nice little talk."

John escorted the lady to a wicker chair, seated himself, and drew out a pack of cigarettes. "Do you mind?"

"No, of course not. My dear Will smoked a pipe, and I loved the smell. These younger women don't appreciate the manly smell of tobacco because so many of them are trying to quit smoking. Nasty habit for a woman. So unladylike."

John lit his cigarette and leaned back in the chair. Polly gave him a thorough inspection, so thorough that he wondered if she were measuring him for a coffin or the auction block. "And just where did you meet my niece, Mr. Mason?"

"In Spring Park yesterday. I was one of her customers at the dunking booth."

"And did you dunk her?"

"Repeatedly," John chuckled at the memory of winning his bet. No doubt, Laurel would not want her aunt to know anything about that.

"Did you come all the way from Ohio just for the Keller Festival?"

"Actually, no. I'm on my way to St. Augustine for a vacation. Tuscumbia is a detour." He debated how much to tell this woman. Perhaps it would be better to explain the situation to her and let her tell Laurel. "My grandmother asked me to do some investigating for her."

"Your grandmother?" Polly folded her small hands in her lap and leaned forward as she asked, "What sort of investigating?"

"A friend of hers who lives in Chattanooga subscribes to the *Observer*, and she sent Gram a copy of Laurel's article about Johnny Drew." John hesitated, wondering how this fragile woman would react to slanderous news about her husband's beloved grandfather. "Well, Mrs. Drew, my grandmother is researching our family tree. And it seems that, uh...that Gram thought Laurel might be able to unearth some facts about an ancestor of ours who supposedly died in this area during the Civil War."

"Really?" Polly's keen silver eyes focused on John's face. "Has Laurel agreed to help you?"

"Well, she did, and she didn't. I don't think your niece quite approves of me."

Polly laughed, and John could almost see the beautiful young girl she once had been. "Mmm...mmm. Laurel has a very romantic nature. When Will and I used to entertain her and her brother, Gene, with tales about Johnny Drew and his Clarice, Laurel would always say that someday, when she was all grown-up, a handsome Yankee would come into her life, and they'd fall madly in love."

John didn't know what to say, didn't know how to respond. So, he thought, my lovely Southern belle has dreamed of a Yankee lover of her own, has she? Well, no doubt, she was sorely disappointed by a hardened sailor who didn't know the first thing about being a dashing gentleman. "Laurel told me that her lifelong dream was to write a biography of Johnny Drew."

"That's true, but I believe the two dreams go together. You do know that her family and this entire town expect her to marry Carter Moody?"

"So she's told me."

"Carter Jackson Moody IV is the most eligible bachelor in the county. Everyone thinks he and Laurel are well suited, a perfect match."

"Something tells me that you don't agree." John took one last draw on his cigarette, and without thinking, threw it onto the porch floor and ground it out with his foot.

"Call me Aunt Polly," the old woman said, a devious smile curling her thin lips. "Carter is handsome, successful, and comes from one of the most prominent families in this state. But the man's a pompous ass. He couldn't even keep that little cow-eyed first wife of his happy. Our Laurel is far too much woman for that jackanapes."

John was delighted by Polly Drew's refreshing candor and pleased that she seemed to like him. He most certainly liked her. "The important thing is, how does Laurel feel about this man?"

"Oh, Laurel isn't fool enough to think herself in love with him, but she is fool enough to listen to that idiot mother of hers, and my henpecked nephew just goes along with it. I'm glad they're gone for the summer on that extended tour of the British Isles. It'll make things easier for you." Polly reached out and poured herself another glass of lemonade. "Would you care for more, John?"

He shook his head "no," amusement warming his dark eyes. "Why are you telling me all this, Mrs., er...Aunt Polly? You wouldn't be conjuring up images of me as Laurel's Yankee lover, would you?"

"I certainly am. I may be old, but I'm not stupid. Do you think I didn't see the way you two were looking at each other? My Lord, there's enough electricity passing between the two of you to light up the whole state of Alabama."

John threw back his head and roared with laughter. Damn, if she hadn't hit the nail squarely on the head. He knew he'd found a comrade in this old woman, possibly someone who'd understand why he'd come to Tuscumbia and why he wasn't prepared to tell Laurel. "Well, Aunt

Polly, I think there's something you should know before you weave too many fantasies. My grandmother sent me here to prove something that could destroy Laurel's dreams.''

Polly sat up straight in the elaborate wicker chair, her small shoulders tensed. "And just what have you come here to prove, John Mason?''

He considered his options. He could simply leave today without telling anybody, or he could tell Aunt Polly and seek her advice, or he could confess to Laurel and take the chance she'd hate him. He decided his best bet was to confide in Polly Drew who seemed wholehcartedly in favor of him romancing her niece.

"I've come here to prove that Johnny Drew and my own great-great-grandfather, J. T. Andrews, is one and the same man.'' John didn't continue. He thought he should give Laurel's aunt a few minutes to assimilate the information.

Polly sat quietly for several minutes, took dainty sips of lemonade, and then faced her guest. "I'm sure that's possible. After all, everyone knows that Johnny Drew deserted the Union army in 1862, and with the DuBois family's help was able to keep that a secret for many years. But in the heart of Dixie, it wasn't considered a dishonorable crime. In fact, it made him quite a hero.''

"I'm afraid, if my suspicions are true, Johnny Drew was more than an army deserter.'' John didn't want to tell this sweet old lady a truth that could upset her and destroy Laurel's chance of immortalizing her Civil War hero.

"What else was he?'' Polly's words were spoken as reverently as if she'd been quoting scriptures in church.

"When J. T. Andrews left Ohio to join the Union army, he left behind a pregnant young bride.''

"No!'' The exclamation came from Laurel who stood in the doorway, her beautiful face flushed with anger. "That's a lie! A man like Pappy Drew would never have done such a thing. He loved Clarice. He worshipped her. He would never, ever have married her if he already had a wife.''

"Laurel." John couldn't bear the look in her eyes. There was hurt and anger reflected in their amethyst depths, but there was betrayal there, too, and he knew he was the one who had betrayed her, not Johnny Drew.

"How can you just sit there listening to these lies?" Laurel demanded as she hurled herself out of the doorway. She stopped in front of John, her hands clenched tightly in fists. "What proof do you have? Don't you have any idea what harm your silly stories could do?"

"Laurel, honey, please calm down." John took her wrists in his hands, bringing her tightened fists between their bodies. When Laurel jerked, trying to free herself, John held her tighter. "I don't have any proof. That's why I'm here. I came to ask you to help me find out the truth."

Polly Drew stood, brushed the wrinkles from her skirt, and loudly cleared her throat. When neither John nor Laurel took any notice of her, Polly cleared her throat again, even louder.

"Let me go," Laurel said in a tone that brooked no argument.

"Will you listen to me," John said, glaring down at the woman trying so hard to pull away from him.

"No. I don't want to hear anything you have to say. I want you to leave. Leave our home. Leave Tuscumbia. Leave this state." Laurel choked back the tears moistening her eyes and clogging her throat.

"Oh, honey, I can't leave. Not now." John wished that he could take back every word, that he could take away the pain his revelation had caused.

Polly cleared her throat one more time, then stomped her tiny foot. "Don't be an idiot, Laurel Drew. All John wants is the truth, and the truth won't hurt any of us unless it should. Help him find out exactly what connection there is between J. T. Andrews and Johnny Drew."

"There is no connection!" Laurel practically screamed.

"Then prove it," Polly said. "You've got all the family records at your disposal, and we've still got Grandmother Clarice's old trunk that we've never completely emptied. Who knows, maybe John's appearance here at this time is providence. Perhaps he'll help you find out things that will make your book even better."

"Finding out that Johnny Drew was a bigamist would ruin my biography," Laurel said, brushing tears from her cheeks with a hand still shackled by John's. "Oh, mercy, this has got to be a nightmare."

"Ms. Drew," the young entry hostess called from the back door. "I'm sorry to bother you, but there's another group ready for the tour."

"You two need to talk." Polly patted her niece on the shoulder. "I'll play hostess for this group while y'all discuss our little problem like civilized people."

Neither John nor Laurel spoke until they were alone on the veranda. When Laurel jerked on her captured hands, John released them. They stood silently staring at each other.

John wanted to pull her into his arms, to comfort her, to promise her that he'd never mention ol' J.T. again. But he knew Laurel would probably slap his face if he tried to hold her, and that there was no way under the sun she was going to pretend he hadn't accused her beloved Johnny Drew of being a bigamist.

When the voices of tourists still sightseeing in the gardens alerted Laurel to the fact that she and John had little privacy here on the veranda, she acted on impulse. She grabbed him by the hand and pulled him with her inside the house. Even though John was surprised by her behavior, he followed Laurel without protest. Once inside, she led him through the modernized kitchen into a small, dark pantry. Before closing the door, she flipped on a light switch, and the pale glow from a 40-watt bulb eliminated the total blackness.

"I want your promise that you won't breathe a word of what you told Aunt Polly and me today." Realizing she still held John's hand, Laurel dropped it as if it were on fire.

"I have no intention of broadcasting ancient history. All I ever wanted to do was find out if ol' J.T. died in the war, or changed his name and lived out the rest of his life as Johnny Drew."

"Quit saying that!" Laurel paced back and forth in the close confines of the tiny room.

"Don't you think you're over-reacting just a little? We're talking about people who lived and died before our parents were even born."

"I wouldn't expect someone like you to understand." Anger and agitation built slowly within Laurel. Her head hurt, her eyes burned with unshed tears, and her heart ached as she saw a lifetime of dreams fade away.

"What do you mean, 'someone like me?' "

"A rough, crude sailor with a tattoo on his arm and a woman in every port."

"You left out one thing." John took several steps toward her, his chest almost brushing her breasts.

"What?" Laurel refused to allow him to intimidate her. She would not back down. She would not give an inch. "Oh, yes, I forgot to add that you're not a gentleman of any kind. That you're the type who's interested in cold beers and hot women. Does that about cover it?"

"You're still forgetting one thing."

"What?" Laurel suddenly felt very hot herself as John moved one step closer. Her breasts pushed into his hard chest, and only the fullness of her hoopskirt prevented her legs from rubbing against his.

"You're forgetting the worst insult of all." He could feel her rapid heartbeat when he lay one hand over her breast.

Laurel knew she should slap his hand away, but she didn't. "The worst insult?" she gasped when John let one finger move slowly down the cleft between her breasts.

"You haven't called me a damn Yankee yet." His finger absorbed the moisture glistening on the tantalizing skin he touched. He pulled his finger up, spreading the dampness to the hollow of her throat.

Laurel's entire body grew taut, and she whimpered softly as her teary eyes met his smoldering ebony ones.

"Are you afraid to call me a Yankee, Laurel? Afraid to admit that I could be to you what Johnny Drew was to Clarice?"

Laurel's lips trembled, and for one moment she couldn't speak. "My...my Yankee...lover?"

She would never know what possessed her to do what she did next. Laurel grabbed John Mason's ruggedly handsome face in both hands, drew his head downward, and pressed her lips against his.

At first he was too shocked to react, but once his body recognized the fact that Laurel was kissing him, he pulled her into his arms and took charge of the situation. When he ran his tongue along her bottom lip, Laurel sighed, opening her mouth enough to invite him inside. And when he took her up on the invitation, she clung to him, her slender hands grasping his shirtfront.

"God, you're hot. Hot and wet and sweet." If her mouth was this wonderful, what would the rest of her be like? He wanted to know, needed to know the secrets of her womanly body. He had never wanted a woman the way he wanted Laurel. It was as if he'd been waiting a lifetime, maybe two lifetimes, to find this violet-eyed temptress.

"I want you...want you..." John moaned against her neck. While his strong arms held her securely, his tongue began a downward slide from her collarbone to the rise of one ripe breast.

"John," Laurel sighed, her fingers weaving through the chest hairs exposed by his open shirt. She had no memory of having unbuttoned the top three buttons, but her fingers hadn't needed her permission to act on impulse. "Johnny...my Johnny."

Aunt Polly's voice penetrated through the closed door as she explained to the guests that this room had not been the original kitchen, that it was located in the basement, and had been left virtually unchanged since Etienne Dubois's time.

"Oh!" Laurel released her hold on John, pulling herself out of his embrace. "I'm sorry. Truly, I'm sorry. I didn't mean for this...I don't know what came over me. Please..."

"It's all right, honey. We're just two people who happen to want each other badly." John reached out to draw her back into his arms.

Laurel stepped backward, her hand clutching the doorknob. "Please, John, go away. Get out of my life and leave me alone. I don't want you. I don't need you."

John didn't try to stop her when she opened the pantry door and stepped into the kitchen. He stood in the doorway and watched while she ran past the roomful of astonished tourists and a smiling Aunt Polly.

"You mustn't miss the tour of the pantry," John said to the crowd. Some of them were staring at him while others were still looking out into the hallway where Laurel had made her hasty exit. "It has a very interesting history, doesn't it, Aunt Polly?"

"Why, yes. Yes, it does. There's an old family tale that Clarice and Johnny once actually made love in there," Aunt Polly lied magnificently.

John walked into the hall and called Laurel's name. He saw her pause briefly about halfway up the staircase.

"I plan to stay on in Tuscumbia for a while, Miss Drew. I'm eager for another tour of the pantry." And I'm eager to hear you call me Johnny when I lose myself inside you, he thought. And I promise that you'll know it's a flesh and blood man making love to you and not some fantasy hero.

Laurel ran the rest of the way up the stairs, not once looking back.

Four

Laurel held the pencil within her closed fist as she sat at the library table and scanned the page of her open book. I'm wasting my time, she thought as the words began to blur. She checked her watch and stuck the end of her pencil in her mouth. Realizing it was already eleven-thirty and she wasn't half finished with her research, Laurel contemplated calling Carter to cancel their lunch date. After all, she was fairly sure she knew what Carter wanted to discuss. He'd been less than subtle when he called and told her that the whole town was talking about her carrying-on with the Yankee stranger.

She had decided that having lunch with Carter today would serve a double purpose—she'd have a sensible person with whom to discuss this whole mess so that she could put the encounter in the proper perspective, and it was something pleasant she could tell her mother the next time Gertrude phoned from Europe and asked about her relationship with Carter.

She had no idea if John Mason had left town or not. She sincerely hoped he had. After what had happened yesterday, she prayed she'd never see the man again. Unfortunately she had no control over her subconscious mind, which allowed him to sneak into her dreams last night. Dreams from which she'd awakened hot and trembling and . . . unfulfilled.

Laurel chewed on the pencil, leaving teeth prints up and down its surface.

"If you're that hungry, maybe you should go on over to the restaurant and eat some real food," the soft-spoken young woman standing beside Laurel said.

"What?"

"You're gnawing on that pencil as if you're starving to death," Bonnie Jean Harland said as she sat down beside Laurel. "All this research getting to you or is your mind wandering?"

"Bonnie Jean, what are you talking about?" Laurel asked as she lay the pencil beside her notebook. "And what are you doing in the library at this time of day?"

"I came by to pester you. Anyway, you aren't fooling me, gal. I saw you with that big, blond hunk Saturday, and word has it that he showed up at the old homestead yesterday for the tour." Bonnie Jean smiled as she crossed her ankle over a blue jean-clad knee in a most unladylike gesture.

"Where did you hear that?" Laurel realized that she should have known the news about her tête-à-tête with John Mason in the pantry would be all over Tuscumbia by now. What were people thinking? How would she ever explain this to her parents?

"You know how word gets around. One old busybody tells another and then she tells another." Bonnie Jean twined her fingers through a strand of her ash blond hair. "Personally, if I ever got a hunk like that alone in a dark pantry, I'd never run out and leave him all alone."

"Well, whoever told you this certainly didn't leave anything out!" Laurel closed her research book so loudly that several library patrons turned to stare at her.

"Actually, they left out the most interesting details because they didn't know them."

Laurel frowned, narrowing her violet eyes as she stared at her friend.

Bonnie Jean laughed, the sound as robust and feminine as the woman herself. "I don't know what happened while you two were in the pantry. You wouldn't care to enlighten me, would you?"

"Bonnie Jean." Laurel's voice rose an octave, then lowered on a muted sigh. "Oh, flitter, I don't know what happened."

"That good, huh?"

"Good? I don't know if good is the right word to describe how I feel. I . . . I've never known anybody like him. Something about him reminds me of Scott, but he's not some redneck college football hero out to—"

"Forget that jerk. He's your ancient history. This big Yankee is nothing like Scott Baker."

"How do you know?"

"Instinct. This guy was looking at you as if you were his favorite dessert and he hadn't tasted any in a long, long time."

"What were you doing, following us?"

"Actually, I was. That and enjoying Carter's outrage. God almighty, gal, why don't you get rid of that man. The only thing ol' Moody IV sees when he looks at you is generations of proper breeding."

"That's another thing I don't understand," Laurel said loudly, then lowered her voice when she heard several discreet coughs coming from around the room. "Why can't you and Carter get along? It can't be just because of your . . . er . . . your relationship with his uncle."

"My relationship with Wheeler Yancey is none of Carter's business, or anybody else's for that matter."

"This is a small town and people talk."

"People like C. J. Moody IV, that...that ancestor worshipping pea-brain."

"Would you like to hear some of the adjectives Carter uses to describe you?" Laurel asked, but had no intention of ever repeating any of the descriptive words Carter used whenever Bonnie Jean Harland's name was mentioned.

"Oh, let me see. Not our kind. Scum. Cheap. White trash. Am I getting close?"

"I know Carter can be a bit narrow-minded, but I've never known him to bad-mouth anyone the way he does you."

"Forget C.J. We were discussing your good-looking Yankee."

"He is not my Yankee," Laurel said, practically hissing each word.

"He hasn't left town, you know."

"What? How do you know?"

Bonnie Jean leaned back in the wooden chair, tipping the front legs off the floor. "Because he's standing in the door and looking straight at us."

Without thinking Laurel turned around and gasped as her gaze locked with his. She found herself drowning in the obsidian depths of John Mason's eyes.

"Oh, my God," Laurel groaned under her breath as she picked up her pencil and absentmindedly rubbed it between the palms of her hands.

"He's coming this way," Bonnie Jean whispered. "I'll make myself scarce."

"No. Don't go." Laurel dropped the pencil on the floor as she reached out to grab her friend's arm.

"Uh...oh. You've got it bad, gal, if you're afraid to be alone with him."

"Hello, Laurel." John Mason stood beside her chair, his big body blocking everything else from view. Laurel swallowed before looking up at him.

When she didn't say anything, John spoke. "Aunt Polly told me you were here. I was hoping we could talk."

"Hey, I was just leaving," Bonnie Jean said as she stood up.

"No," Laurel said.

"I've got to get back to work." Bonnie Jean winked at Laurel, smiled at John, and walked away. "I'll call you later."

John stepped on the pencil lying on the floor beside Laurel's chair. "Your pencil?"

"Yes," she replied and bent to retrieve it.

John had the same idea at the exact same moment. Laurel could feel his breath on her neck. She knew his face was directly behind her. When she reached for the pencil, John's hand touched hers. She grabbed the pencil in trembling fingers, fingers covered by John's. As she moved her body upright again, she turned her face and found his scant inches away.

"Oh," she breathed, her lips almost brushing his.

"Laurel." The way he said her name was hypnotic. She felt herself sway toward him, her heart reaching out.

Laurel pulled her hand away from him, wondering how she could break the spell his nearness was weaving around her. Suddenly remembering the pencil in her hand, she stuck it behind her ear and accidently grazed John's cheek with the lead tip.

Instinctively he moved backward a few inches. He looked at Laurel and saw fear in her eyes. He didn't want her to be afraid of him, but he had to admit that male instinct told him her fear was totally sexual.

The proper, very beautiful Ms. Drew was as attracted to him as he was to her, and she was afraid of where that attraction might lead. John knew where *he* wanted it to lead—

into his arms and into his bed. He'd spent another night tossing and turning, trying to catch a few hours of sleep without being haunted by dreams of a black-haired mermaid.

Laurel pulled the pencil from behind her ear and picked up her notebook. Trying to calm the butterflies in her stomach, she took a deep breath and turned to face him. "What are you doing here?"

John pulled out a chair and sat down beside her. "I want to talk to you. I think we need to straighten out this mess about ol' J.T. and your Pappy Drew."

Laurel quickly surveyed the room to see if anyone had overheard. "Hush. We don't have anything to talk about. We said everything yesterday." She glared at him and saw him smiling at her. His smile reminded her of another smile. She shut her eyes tightly and shook her head, then reopened her eyes.

"Why are you being so pigheaded about this? I'd think a historian on the verge of having her first book published would be interested in the complete truth about her subject."

"I already know the complete truth. I don't know who this J.T. Andrews was, but he wasn't my great-great-grandfather," she whispered, her cheeks flushing and her body tensing as she leaned toward him. His smile had disappeared, but the image of that other smile remained in Laurel's mind—the smile captured on canvas long ago by some forgotten painter. How many times had she longingly looked at that portrait?

John scooted his chair closer to her and bent his head, their gazes tangling in direct confrontation. "You're probably right. Look, all I'm asking for is a little of your time."

"I—"

"Hey, not for me, but for my grandmother. This ancestor stuff means a lot to her." John knew he was stretching the truth a bit, but he didn't care if it won him more time with Laurel.

She clenched her teeth as she looked at John and shook her head in a negative response. She didn't dare spend any more time with this man. People were already talking. Not only was he a Yankee, but he was a roughneck, and they obviously had nothing in common. If only she could erase the image of Johnny Drew's sensual smile—the identical smile she'd seen on John Mason's rugged face.

"Give me a couple of hours today," John said, his black eyes pleading. "Let me take you to lunch and then we'll spend the afternoon together. How about it?"

She wanted to say "yes." Every female instinct within her yearned to share with this man, this big, hard man who made her insides quiver with excitement. She wondered if Johnny Drew had made Clarice DuBois feel this way. "I...I don't know. This is a small town, and people are already talking. Besides, I have—"

"Laurel." He wasn't going to allow her to refuse him. There was something going on between the two of them that was too good to ignore. He couldn't let her apprehensions stop him, even if it meant forcing her to face the truth.

Why didn't he go away? she wondered. He was making her act like a silly little girl. Why couldn't the man take no for an answer? If she spent more time with him, she'd be lost in the dream of her heart. She knew she couldn't allow herself to start thinking of John Mason as her fantasized Yankee lover. "I already have a lunch date."

"With Carter Jackson Moody IV?"

"As a matter of fact, yes." Politeness and subconscious need overruled her better judgment when she blurted out, "You're welcome to join us, if you'd like."

"Thanks, I'd love to." John smiled, the predatory gleam in his eyes issuing a challenge.

Oh, Lordy, what have I done? Laurel asked herself. Good ol' Carter would have a fit; the whole town would be discussing the event by nightfall, and she had just condemned herself to spending more time with a man who tempted her beyond reason. "We're eating over at Bonnie Jean's. It's one of the best places in town to eat."

"Bonnie Jean's?"

"The woman who was with me when you came in," Laurel said. "She owns The Plantation restaurant down on Main Street."

"A fancy place?"

"No, not at all." Laurel laughed, remembering the night she helped Bonnie Jean come up with the name for the place. "It's located in an old building downtown, and she serves good old-fashioned Southern food."

"I can hardly wait."

"I... er... I need to finish up here first." Laurel opened her book, turned several pages, and scribbled a few hasty, incoherent notes. She simply couldn't keep her mind on her research. All she could think about was sharing lunch with John Mason. Everyone in town would know.

John sat watching her, savoring the sight of her golden body in a pair of white walking shorts and neat pink gingham blouse. Ever the lady, he thought. Although her alluring body and beautiful face enticed a man's thoughts to border on the obscene, her genteel manner filled his heart with some odd notions. Notions of holding hands, and sweet kisses, and gentle touches.

He couldn't take his eyes off her as she wrote furiously in the thick notebook. Suddenly she stopped writing, put the pencil back behind her ear, and started rubbing the back of her neck with both hands. When she sighed, her full pink mouth opened and she licked her bottom lip. John felt his heart lurch and his maleness tighten. He wanted to touch her.

Laurel studied the pages of her research book but had no idea what she was reading. It was useless to try to finish her work with John Mason sitting beside her watching her like a hawk circling a chicken. She increased the pressure of her hands at her neck, their nervous movements evidence of the tumult raging inside her.

Suddenly John grabbed her by the shoulders. Laurel gasped and stared at him as if he'd lost his mind.

"What?" she asked, the puzzlement in her voice reflected in her lavender-blue eyes.

John took several deep breaths, his chest expanding and contracting as he forced his body under control. What? she'd asked. What? Well, if he told her what, she'd faint at his feet. No well-bred Southern lady would like to be told a man wanted to ravish her in the middle of a public library. "Isn't it about time for lunch?"

Yes, Laurel thought, early or not, it's definitely time for lunch. Perhaps Carter's presence would defuse the time bomb ticking between John and her. "Sure."

He stood and waited for her to replace the book on the shelf and gather her notebook. "After lunch, will you give me an hour at least?" he asked.

"I'll give you a tour of the town," she said as they walked toward the door. "We'll come up with something to tell your grandmother so you can be on your way to that Florida vacation by tomorrow."

He opened the door for her and stood back watching the feminine sway of her hips as she moved past him. "You're in a hurry to see me leave town."

She hesitated briefly, halting her steps to turn and look at him. "There's nothing in Tuscumbia for you. There's no reason for you to stay."

"Maybe, maybe not." He put his hand, palm open against her back, and felt a slight tremor pass through her body before she started walking again. She stopped beside a sleek, silver Mark VII, opened the door and tossed her notebook inside. "You can follow me to The Plantation."

"Why don't you leave your car here, and we can both go in mine."

"I . . . well, okay." She wanted to decline his offer but couldn't think of one logical reason to do so.

The Plantation wasn't quite what John had expected, even after Laurel's appraisal of the restaurant. It was located in a very old building, and the food was definitely Southern. The smell of hot corn bread filled his nostrils as he tore another piece apart and tossed it into his mouth. The only thing about the place that was reminiscent of a Southern plantation, however, was a picture of a manor house on the front of the menu.

"Laurel tells me you're on your way to Florida for a vacation, Mr. Mason." Carter set his coffee cup on the table.

"That's right." John swallowed a mouthful of food before answering. "I've got an old Navy buddy down there. He owns a boating business. Wants to show me around."

"Our little town is flattered that you'd stop by here for our festival." Carter's crystal-blue eyes showed no emotion.

"Actually, I didn't—" John began speaking.

"He heard the announcement on the radio while he was driving." Laurel couldn't let John reveal the real reason he'd come to Tuscumbia. "You'll have to tell the committee that radio advertising really works."

John lifted the iced-tea glass to his lips. She may be involved with this guy, John thought, but she doesn't trust him enough to tell him the truth. Is she afraid gentlemanly Carter would print the sordid details on the front page of his weekly paper?

"How long are you planning on staying around?" Carter asked politely.

Hmm . . . mmm, John thought, this guy's no dummy. He may be a gentleman, but he's just issued me a warning. Well, maybe he'd misjudged the man. Maybe, just maybe, there was more to Carter Jackson Moody IV than met the eye. "I'm in no hurry."

"Jo...Mr. Mason will probably be on his way by tomorrow," Laurel said, touching Carter on the arm and smiling at him. "I'm going to give him a tour of the town after lunch."

"Sort of a farewell gift, my dear?" Carter asked, a plastic smile on his handsome face.

Laurel kept smiling at Carter, thankful for his impeccable manners. But then, what could he do, challenge John to a duel? It wasn't as if she were Carter's woman, even if the whole town thought she should be.

She sipped her tea, allowing a couple of pieces of ice to slide into her mouth. While she mused about the outcome of a fight between her two unlikely heroes, Laurel began to munch. She could picture Carter in Confederate gray with a saber in his hand. Then the image of John Mason, dirty and unkempt from days on the road, filled her mind. He was a dashing Yankee lieutenant with a smile that could tempt a Southern belle's heart.

John watched and listened as Laurel crunched on the ice. He grinned when he saw the look of stern disapproval on Carter's face. Carter cleared his throat several times before gaining Laurel's attention. He widened his eyes, giving her a that's-bad-etiquette stare. She deliberately swallowed the ice.

"Dessert, anybody?" Bonnie Jean's distinctive Southern voice drawled.

John couldn't help but notice the tensing in Carter's body and the ashen pallor of his complexion. It was apparent that this Bonnie Jean stirred some pretty deep emotions in Laurel's boyfriend.

"Running short of waitresses?" Carter asked, but kept his eyes fixed on his plate.

Bonnie Jean's laugh sounded oddly sad. "I wanted to give special service to special customers. It isn't every day that Laurel has lunch with a good-looking Yankee."

"Mr. Mason is our guest," Carter said, tightening his jaw but still refusing to look directly at their attractive hostess.

"Well, that's even more special." Bonnie Jean stepped closer to Carter, the side of her hip brushing against his arm.

"I'd love some cherry cobbler," Laurel said. "You should try some, John. It's delicious."

"Make that two," John said.

"What about you, C.J.? You in the mood for a little something sweet?" Bonnie Jean nudged Carter with her hip.

"Just more coffee." Carter pronounced each word distinctly.

"Dessert's on the house," Bonnie Jean said as she left their table.

"God, what an offensive woman!" Carter groaned as he clenched his linen napkin in his hand and threw it on the table.

"Really, Carter, I don't know why you dislike her so much. She's one of the nicest people I've ever known, even if she did come from Sugar Hill. She can't help who her people are." Laurel didn't want to have this discussion in front of John Mason. He probably had no idea about the fine line separating the social classes in a small Southern town. He'd never understand.

"This is hardly the time or place to discuss that woman." Carter nodded his head in the direction of Bonnie Jean's exit.

"Well, well, Carter, dear boy. And Laurel." A hefty woman in her late sixties approached their table, a pen and notepad in her hand. "This is simply perfect. Y'all are entertaining Mr. Mason, I see."

Oh, Lord, please no, Laurel thought. Of all people on earth to run into. Mabel Suggs was the busiest busybody in town, and a reporter for the *Colbert Daily News*. The woman's 'People Talk' column was read by every concerned citizen in the county.

"Mabel," Carter gulped. "How nice to see you."

"May I join y'all?" Mabel asked. "I do want to interview Mr. Mason for my column. Polly tells me that you think an ancestor of yours died in these parts during the war." The portly Mrs. Suggs sat in the vacant chair between Laurel and John.

"What?" Carter glared at Laurel.

"Dessert." Bonnie Jean interrupted long enough to set the cobbler bowls on the table and motion for a waitress to refill Carter's coffee cup. "Well, hello, Mrs. Suggs. Would you care for coffee or dessert?"

"Coffee," the older woman said, and the waitress set a cup before her immediately.

"Mind if I listen to this interview?" Bonnie Jean pulled up a chair from a nearby table and sat down between Carter and John.

"I'm afraid I don't understand all the interest in one Yankee visitor," John told them, realizing that Laurel probably wanted to kill him. She looked as if one wrong word would topple her over the edge.

Mabel giggled, actually giggled like a little girl. "It's not every day that our Laurel takes a personal interest in helping a Northerner do genealogical research." The columnist opened her pad. "Where are you from, Mr. Mason?"

"Who told you I was helping John?" Immediately Laurel regretted using his given name. Everyone would be reading more into that slip of the tongue than they should.

"Polly, of course," Mabel said. "She seems to think you have something to worry about, Carter."

I'm going to kill her, Laurel thought. My own aunt, and she's probably told the whole world that I... She refused to allow the thought to continue.

"Oh, you know what a romantic Aunt Polly is." Laurel turned to Mrs. Suggs, hoping to remedy some of the damage her aunt's ravings had caused.

"I'd say Aunt Polly was right about one thing." Bonnie Jean looked at Carter, a smugly satisfied expression crossing her face. "With a real man like Johnny around, the oh-so-honorable Mr. Moody has more competition than he can handle."

"Look, Mrs. Suggs," John said as he stood up. "Laurel's giving me a tour of the town, and she's going to look up some family information for my grandmother. That's all there is to it. And I think we should get started if I'm going to make my two o'clock appointment."

Laurel lay her napkin on the table and stood up. "You're right. Sorry, everybody, but we have to run. Mabel, I promise to tell you everything, later."

Carter looked up at Laurel and nodded. "Don't forget that we're expecting Aunt Polly and you for dinner tonight."

"I won't forget."

"You and Mr. Mason have a pleasant afternoon," Carter said.

The moment the restaurant doors closed behind her, Laurel felt an overwhelming sense of relief. "Thank you. I didn't know how we were going to get out of that one. Mabel is like a dog with a bone. Once she gets wind of gossip, she sinks her teeth in and holds on for dear life."

John wanted to put his arms around Laurel and tell her that he never wanted to be the cause of embarrassment or pain for her. Instead, he led her to the car. When he opened the door, she turned to him and smiled. He smiled back and both of them burst into laughter.

He helped her into his car, closed his eyes briefly, and made a silent wish. He promised himself not to rush her today. All he wanted was a chance to set things right, to open the door for tomorrow.

Three hours later, John parked his Jag on a small dirt lane less than a mile away from the DuBois-Drew Home. After Laurel gave him the thirty-minute tour of Tuscumbia, she'd agreed to show him around the whole of Colbert County.

They'd driven from the east end near Leighton to the west end near the Mississippi border. It amazed him that so much of the land was being cultivated, and King Cotton still grew in the Southland. He and Laurel had talked about everything except Johnny Drew.

John turned to look at her as she lay her head back on the leather seat and gazed up at the blue sky. She's so beautiful, he thought, so very beautiful. He wanted to reach out and touch her face, to tell her what just the sight of her did to him.

Laurel breathed in the fresh, warm air and smiled as she turned her head toward John. Her smile broadened when she looked at him.

"I've enjoyed this afternoon," she admitted to herself as much as to him. "Even though I should have been at the library finishing my research, I'm glad we had today together."

He reached out and touched her cheek, his finger tracing the outline of her face. "I don't want the day to end," he said, watching her intently.

"It has to end." She pulled away from him, shaking her head. "You'll be leaving for Florida tomorrow, won't you?"

"Yeah, I guess I should, but I—"

"What will you tell your grandmother?"

"I don't know." He knew Laurel was deliberately trying not to look at him. "That I couldn't find out anything, I guess."

"If I . . . if I helped you find out about this J.T. Andrews and he . . . well, if . . ." She couldn't believe what she was saying. She was actually thinking about helping this man find out a truth that could possibly destroy a dream she'd cherished all her life. If Johnny Drew was a bigamist, she'd never be able to publish his biography.

"If it turns out that my grandmother's suspicions are true, there's no need for anyone else to ever know."

"I'm not sure I'm ready to take that kind of risk." She weighed her two choices carefully in her mind. She could send John away and never find out the truth. Or she could ask him to stay until they proved his story true or false. If he left, she could finish her book, keep her dreams alive, and continue her life as she'd planned. If he stayed, she'd be gambling with her whole life—her dreams, her plans, her book. And her heart. If John stayed, how long could she resist him?

"I don't want to leave." He wanted to pull her into his arms and hold her, but he'd promised himself to go slow. A woman like Laurel needed to be courted, and even if he didn't know a damned thing about wooing a lady, he knew that Laurel might need time, and he was willing to give her all the time she needed. It might kill him, but he'd do it.

"Do you promise me that no matter what we find out, it will remain a secret? It's not just me. It's my family, and the whole town."

"I promise." He would have promised her anything just to have her agree to see him again. If the only leverage he had was ol' J.T., he had no scruples about using him. John wanted Laurel Drew more than he'd ever wanted another woman, and even though she was out of his league, he was determined to have her.

"We'll spend as much time as I can spare going through all the records." The thought of spending hours, even days with John Mason made her body tingle with an excitement that both exhilarated and frightened her. "As soon as we can prove that Johnny Drew and J.T. Andrews were two different men, you'll leave and never tell a soul about your grandmother's theory?"

"How long do you think it will take?" he asked, wondering just how much time he'd have to win her heart. If he made a fool of himself over Laurel, so be it. He hadn't taken a chance on a woman since he'd been twenty-one and fallen head-over-heels in love with his commanding officer's daughter, Cassie Whitson. Laurel might seem just as unattainable as Cassie had been, but Laurel was a grown woman who could choose for herself the man she wanted.

"This...this thing between us, John..." She had decided to be honest.

John could feel his heart beating like a jackhammer. He tried to smile at her, but she still wasn't looking at him. He took her chin in his hand and turned her face upward. "Look at me, Laurel."

She looked up into his eyes, and the desire she saw reflected there stunned her. This was a man with primitive emotions, basic needs, and a male strength that called to the female softness in her. "Nothing can happen between us. Do you understand?" she said gently.

His hold on her jaw tightened slightly but not painfully. "No, I don't understand. Something has already happened between us. Something powerful."

"You're wrong for me," she said in a rush. "We're wrong for each other. I will not let this attraction I feel for you overrule my better judgment."

"I think what you're trying to tell me is that I'm not good enough for you. Hell, you're probably right, but it doesn't stop me from wanting you." He released his hold on her and lowered his head until his lips almost touched hers. "Come down off that pedestal, lady, and find out what it's like with a man instead of a gentleman."

"I did that once, and it was a disaster." Laurel choked back the tears as she dropped her head and covered her face with her hands.

John felt as if she'd slapped him. The thought that some fool had hurt Laurel made him want to kill. "Don't make me pay for another man's sins. Whoever this other guy was, he obviously didn't feel for you what I do."

Laurel raised her head and wiped the tears from her face. "Drive me back to the library. I need to pick up my car."

"Laurel?"

"If you can stay a few days, that should be long enough to clear things up."

"Fine. I'll call Nate and tell him I'll be delayed." He decided there wasn't much he could do right now but play the game by her rules. She'd given him a few days, and by God, he intended to make the most of them. Days had a way of turning into weeks, and weeks into a lifetime.

Five

Laurel stood in the middle of Clarice DuBois Drew's sitting room, looking at the portraits hanging above the fireplace. The artist had captured the beauty of a girl in the bloom of youth, her ebony hair fashionably netted, her brown eyes glowing with life. The other canvas showed a man on the verge of maturity, his golden hair long, his mustache trimmed, and a sadly wise gleam in his blue-violet eyes. Laurel had seen these pictures countless times during her life, and now, as each time before, her mind began to weave fantasies of love and passion.

John Mason had been in town almost a week, and she'd seen him for a few hours every day. Although they had unearthed no new facts about Johnny Drew, they had learned some things about each other and the vast differences in their lives and their future plans. She'd been able to keep her feelings for John under control, and she had to admit that he'd tried hard to keep their relationship as casual as she'd told him she wanted.

She'd seen Carter once since she and Aunt Polly had dined with his family. It had been a bittersweet meeting for both of them. When she'd told him that she felt it best if they didn't date anymore, Carter warned her that she was making a mistake to become involved with a Yankee stranger whose lack of breeding was so obvious. She'd agreed with him and assured him that she had no intention of having an affair with John Mason. Laurel knew that despite his big-brother protectiveness, Carter was as relieved as she was to finally end their going-nowhere relationship.

Perhaps if John Mason had never entered her life, she could have grown to love Carter as more than a friend. He was a gentleman, and yet he was all man. She couldn't understand why the touch of his hands or the feel of his lips were only pleasant sensations when one look from John melted her heart.

Had Clarice loved Johnny with mindless passion? Laurel wondered. When he'd looked at her, had she turned to flame?

"Well, Pappy, were you J. T. Andrews? Did you leave behind a pregnant wife? Did your beloved Clarice know?" Laurel asked the portrait of her great-great-grandfather.

"How would you feel if the answer to all those questions is yes?" Polly Drew stood in the open doorway, a basket of pink roses in her hand.

"Oh. I didn't know you were there," Laurel said as she turned to face her great-aunt. "I was just thinking out loud."

"Sometimes the dead bury their secrets with them." Polly walked into the room and set her basket on a Queen Anne tea table near the window. "You and John may never know the truth."

"You think Pappy Drew really was this J. T. Andrews, don't you?"

Polly stood by the window, her fingers caressing the tassel-trimmed draperies. "I think it's quite possible, even probable."

"But why?" Laurel asked, wondering if Aunt Polly knew more than she was telling.

"Because I've lived long enough to know human nature, to understand men and women and love. Oh, my sweet girl, we do totally mad, impulsive things when we're in love." Polly took her niece's hand and squeezed tightly.

"But what about honesty and honor and tradition?"

"Fine words. Noble sentiments. But you've never been in love, Laurel." When Laurel started to speak, her aunt raised a hand to silence her. "Hush. That little interlude you had in college had nothing to do with love, or even passion, for that matter."

"Why on earth did I ever tell you about Scott?" Laurel turned away from her aunt's scrutiny, her gaze focusing on the scenery outside the window. When she'd told her aunt about her affair with Scott Baker, she'd known the old woman's addiction to gossip didn't extend to revealing secrets that would harm those she loved.

"Because you needed some maternal advice and concern, and you could hardly go to Gertrude and tell her you'd lost your virginity." Polly patted the younger woman on the back. "Besides, you know I can keep a secret when I have to."

Laurel tensed, unpleasant memories bombarding her. "Funny, isn't it? Mother thinks I'm still a virgin. As a matter of fact, I think Carter does, too."

"Pooh on Carter. He's the wrong man for you, and you're the wrong woman for him."

"Except for Carter and me, you're the only person I know who doesn't think we're the perfect couple."

"You're too perfect. The perfect Southern gentleman and his lady. What you need is a rough, slightly crude Yankee."

Laurel felt a twinge of apprehension at her need to share her feelings with someone who'd understand, someone like Aunt Polly. But first, she would have to admit a few things to herself, and she wasn't sure if she was ready to do that. "John Mason frightens me."

"You're used to men who play games, men who always say and do the acceptable thing. But, Laurel, child, being a gentleman doesn't make someone a good man."

"If you're trying to tell me that a man shouldn't be judged on his pedigree, I agree. But—"

"Has Carter ever made you feel the way John does? You idolize your Pappy Drew and his Clarice, and they overcame insurmountable odds because they loved each other. You're their descendant, a part of them." Polly paused for a few moments, her slender arm going around Laurel's shoulder. "And it's quite possible John Mason, too, is a part of Johnny Drew. The same passionate blood may flow in his veins."

Laurel laughed, knotted her hand in a fist, and placed it against her forehead. "And you call me a romantic."

"What's the worst that can happen if you give in to your feelings for John?"

"The worst?" Laurel asked as she walked across the room, picked up her aunt's flower basket, and began removing the roses. "Hmm...mmm, let me think. Well, we'd find out that J. T. Andrews and Johnny Drew were the same man, John would expose that fact to the world, and then he'd go on his merry way to Florida."

"Which would hurt the most, his exposing the truth or his leaving?"

"I...I'm not sure. Both, I guess. Oh, Aunt Polly, he's not the type of man who'll settle for holding hands and a goodnight kiss. He'll want an affair, and I'm...I'm..."

"You're nearly thirty years old, not twenty. It wouldn't be the end of the world if you had an affair."

"Aunt Polly!"

"Oh, don't Aunt Polly me. Any woman who says that sex isn't important in a relationship never had the right kind of relationship. A woman needs a man who makes her heart sing, her body tingle, and her blood run hot."

The insistent ringing of the telephone cut short any reply Laurel would have made.

"You arrange the flowers for me," Aunt Polly said. "I'll answer the phone."

Laurel took the empty crystal vase sitting on the table and walked into the adjoining bathroom. Just as she came out with the water-filled vase, Aunt Polly met her at the door.

"It's John."

"Oh, Aunt Polly, he'll ask me to spend the day with him."

"Then do it. If you don't, you'll live to regret it. Spend the whole day with a man who curls your toes. Forget about who you are, who your family is and was, and forget about Pappy Drew and that darn biography."

"Maybe I could. For just one day."

"Take John to the river house. Y'all can swim and boat and ski. Go tell him, and I'll fix a picnic lunch before he gets here."

Laurel hesitated briefly, trying to consider all the consequences of being reckless. She'd paid dearly once before for taking a chance. But John wasn't Scott, and she wasn't a foolish young girl anymore.

"All right," Laurel said as she rushed out of the sitting room and down the hall to the telephone in her aunt's bedroom.

"Hello," she said breathlessly.

"Laurel."

"How would you like to go on a picnic? My folks have a house on the river, down on Rose Trail. We could spend the day in our bathing suits soaking up Alabama sunshine." The words rushed out of her in a torrent of excitement and anticipation.

"The purple bathing suit you were wearing the first time I saw you?" His voice lowered to a husky male growl.

Laurel felt elated. This was going to be a day out of time, a stolen moment for which she'd have no regrets. "I suppose I could wear that one if you want me to, but I kind of wanted to wear my bikini."

"Bikini?" John asked, a slight vibration in his voice.

"Can you pick me up in an hour?"

"Does fire burn?"

"You do have swim trunks, don't you?"

"Yep."

"Bikini ones?" Her mind filled with the image of John's body in nothing but a pair of bikini briefs. Her respiration quickened and her heartbeat accelerated. She clutched the phone tightly.

"Yep."

John lay on his stomach, his body relaxing into the softness of the old quilt that he and Laurel had spread on the ground. She lay beside him, her eyes closed as her golden flesh soaked in the warmth from the late afternoon sun. His gaze moved slowly from her almost too-beautiful face, down her slender neck to the tempting swell of her barely covered breasts. When she'd said a bikini, she'd meant a bikini. The small strips of black and lavender just barely concealed the most intimate parts of her luscious body. He couldn't help but wonder if Carter Moody had seen her in this little-bit-of-nothing. God, could school teachers actually wear stuff like that these days?

He felt her stir beside him as she arched her leg, her knee pointing skyward. His eyes moved lower, caressing the flat smoothness of her stomach, kissing her tiny, round navel, longing to strip away the minute piece of material that hid her treasures from his view. He forced his gaze to move on, to follow the line of her full, feminine thigh. His hands itched to touch her there, between her soft, tan thighs, to fondle her in gentle exploration.

She took a deep breath, stretching, tossing her arms above her head. Her breasts pushed against their meager covering as if longing to be free. He wanted to remove the frail barrier that kept her beauty from his sight and touch.

"Did you never see your father?" Laurel asked.

It took John several minutes to respond because during his appraisal of her lush assets, he'd forgotten their conversation about his parents. "Nope. He married my mother because she was pregnant and her old man threatened him. Hell, he didn't even wait around long enough to see me christened."

Laurel flipped over on her side, opening her eyes to look directly at him. "Your mother must have been devastated when he left. She was so young. Sixteen."

"I don't know. I don't remember her being anything except a pretty little butterfly who'd kiss me good-night before going off to another party."

"How old were you when she died?"

John let his thoughts go backward in time, trying to remember a woman who wasn't much more than a vague memory. "Ten. But I'd never thought of her as my mother. Gram was the only mother I ever knew."

"You love your grandmother very much, don't you?"

"I'd do just about anything for that old woman. I think she's the only body in my life that's ever truly loved me."

"Oh, John."

He knew he had revealed too much of himself with those few words. The last thing he wanted from Laurel Drew was sympathy. "The one thing Gram wanted the most was for me and the old man to be friends. Hell, maybe we were too much alike. All I can remember is him trying to run my life, telling me what to do."

Laurel wanted to reach out and pull John into her arms, to ease the pain she heard in his voice, to alleviate the hurt he wanted to hide. She couldn't believe another woman hadn't loved him passionately at sometime in his life. Before she could speak, realization of just what she'd been thinking struck her. Another woman. Loved him. Was she admitting to herself that she loved him? But she couldn't allow herself to love John Mason. She couldn't! "Did you and your grandfather ever patch things up?"

"No, not really. I don't think he ever forgave me for joining the Navy straight out of high school instead of going on to college like he'd planned. He was damned and determined for me to make something of myself."

"And you have," Laurel said calmly, but warring emotions raged within her. The more she knew about John, the more she wanted to know. The longer she was in his presence, the deeper her feelings for him became. Every time he looked at her, she wanted to touch him, to ask him to touch her.

"That's debatable. Has anything really changed since I was eighteen? Hell, I didn't know what I really wanted then. To escape the old man, I guess. But here I am, twenty years later, he's dead, and Gram wants me to come home and go into business with my cousin who now owns the meat-packing plant where the old man worked."

"And what do you want to do?" Laurel asked, knowing his relationship with his deceased grandfather was still creating problems for him.

"I love Gram. I owe her a lot. God, I feel so obligated. But I'd been making plans to live in Florida, to go into business with Nate."

"Nate?"

"Nate Hodges, an old Navy buddy of mine. He's a quarter Seminole Indian, half Scotch-Irish, and a quarter wolf."

Laurel laughed, wondering just what kind of man this Nate actually was. "Wolf? As in part animal, or as in a woman-chaser?"

"Both," John said, chuckling at the good memories that always came to mind when he thought about his best friend.

"So you want to go into business with Nate, but your grandmother wants you to stay in Ohio."

"Right."

"Are you and this cousin close?"

"No. We hardly know each other. He's my mother's sister's kid. She married better than my mother. Brett's always been the suit and tie kind."

"Unlike you."

"Yeah, unlike me."

"Why don't you simply be honest with your grandmother?"

"Could you be honest with your mother if you wanted to do something totally opposite of what she wanted for you?" He reached into the pocket of his shirt, which lay at his feet, and pulled out a cigarette pack and lighter.

"Your Gram doesn't sound anything like my mother. She sounds more like Aunt Polly, and I could tell her almost anything."

Laurel didn't like to think about how little her own mother actually knew about her. They were virtual strangers, polite, always cordial strangers who just happened to be mother and daughter. The one thing Gertrude Drew wanted more than anything in this world was to see her only daughter married to Carter Jackson Moody IV.

"Well, we've pretty well dissected my parents, what about yours?" John lit his cigarette and tossed the pack and lighter down on the quilt.

"What do you want to know?" She knew she could pretty well sum up Eugene and Gertrude Drew in a few sentences.

"Aunt Polly said they're off in Europe, right?"

"They're on a tour of the British Isles. Every summer for the past five years, since Daddy retired from his real estate firm, they've taken off somewhere. Usually they wait until after the festival because mother is so involved with numerous local organizations.''

''What organizations?''

''Mmm...mmm, let me see. Friends of the Library, Historical Society, Daughters of the Confederacy, Natchez Trace Genealogical Society, her study club—''

''Never mind,'' John said, placing a hand up in a stop signal. ''What about you, Laurel, do you belong to all these organizations?''

''Oh, yes, as a matter of fact, I do. You see, John, it's a matter of—''

''Who you are,'' he said harshly.

''I'm not going to apologize for my mother or myself for being civic-minded, concerned—''

''Snobs.'' The word was like a gunshot straight to her ears.

Laurel tensed, the muscles in her body grew taut, and her teeth ground together. She took several deep breaths, the anger within her slowly reaching the boiling point. ''Is that what you think of me?'' She jumped up, hands on her hips as she glared down at him.

''Is that what you are, Laurel?''

''No.'' His accusation angered her, but she wondered if perhaps she was a snob, at least partly. Since the first moment she'd seen John, she'd thought he was rough and crude, beneath her socially. A man to be avoided at all costs. If he'd been a member of her social circle, would she have been fighting her attraction to him? She stepped backward when he stood up, his dark eyes boring into hers, demanding a more honest reply.

''I think you're the most beautiful, most desirable woman I've ever known,'' he said truthfully. ''But you scare me, lady. You scare the hell out of me. I've never known anyone like you.'' John crushed his cigarette against the ground.

She desperately wanted to hold him in her arms. Her body ached with a need for his touch. ''I...I've never known anyone like you, either," she said, then ran from him. She ran toward the river, toward the warm depths of the mighty Tennessee. When she reached the wharf's edge, she dived in.

John called her name, and when she didn't respond, he followed her in.

She swam away from him. He pursued his elusive mermaid until he caught her around the waist and dragged her struggling body into his arms.

"No, don't. Let me go," she said, splashing the water around them as she tried to free herself.

"Running away isn't going to stop what you're feeling inside. I didn't mean to hurt your feelings, honey, but I've got to know what's holding you back."

She sighed and leaned into him, her wet, nearly naked body dissolving into the hard, hot strength of his. "I'm more afraid of you than you could possibly be of me. I'm not ready for this . . . for you."

His mouth came down on hers then like a hammer on an anvil, and the sensation pounded through her body with a powerful force. She opened her mouth for his tongue and flung her arms around his neck. Their combined weights dragged them beneath the surface of the water, their bodies sinking as they clung to each other. John ended the kiss, kicked his feet, and brought them to the surface, both of them gasping for air.

"Whew, woman, a man could drown making love to you."

"Only if he tries to do it in the Tennessee River," Laurel laughed, all the anger draining out of her.

"You have a point." He touched her cheek with his lips, a sweet, undemanding kiss that tingled through Laurel like the effects of good wine.

"Are you hungry?" she asked.

He cocked one eyebrow. "Absolutely."

"For food?" She could have bitten off her tongue the minute the words came out of her mouth.

"Of course. What else would I be hungry for?" He smiled a we'll-finish-this-later smile and swam away, leaving Laurel with her mouth agape.

Within ten minutes they had dried off and spread out the picnic lunch Aunt Polly had packed for them. John crunched on a piece of fried chicken while Laurel nibbled on a deviled egg. She tried not to stare at him too much, but she couldn't resist the pleasure.

John Mason had to be the most masculine man she'd ever known. His body was big and muscled. There was a staggering air of virility about him. Every look, every word, every touch called to her on a level far removed from rational thought. It was as if her body knew something she didn't, as if the very thing that made her a woman, knew he was her man.

"How serious are you and this Carter guy?" John asked as he poured more iced tea from the thermos.

She wanted to be honest with John, but she wasn't quite sure if he would see her lack of a committed relationship with Carter as a sign of encouragement. "We . . . we're—"

"You're not in love with him, are you?" John asked, then tilted his glass and downed the cool liquid.

"I'm very fond of Carter. We care about each other. I've known him all my life." Even to her own ears, the words sounded feeble, the emotions lacking in any real depth.

"Is he a good lover?"

"What?" She couldn't believe he'd had the gall to ask her such a question.

"He's a good-looking guy, virile enough, I guess, even if he's a stuck-up Southern gentleman." John hated to admit that Carter Moody could very well be the kind of man who'd appeal to women.

"Carter is a product of his heritage just as I am. I suppose that's why the whole town thinks we're so perfect for each other."

"Are you perfect together, Laurel?" He wondered why he was pressing her to tell him the one thing he couldn't bear to hear. The very thought of her being with another man tore into his gut like a blunt knife.

"I don't think you have a right to ask me such personal questions. After all, I haven't asked you about all the women in your past or present." Laurel picked up a roll and tore it into tiny pieces. What would he think if he knew she'd never made love with Carter, that she'd only had one lover? she wondered. Would he laugh? Would he find her inadequate the way Scott had?

"You're the only woman in my present. And all you have to do is ask and I'll tell you anything you want to know about my past," John wiped his hands on the red gingham napkin laying across his bare legs.

"I don't know if we have that much time," she said, and instantly regretted the sharp tone of her voice.

"Look, honey, I've known my share of women. I won't deny the fact." He tucked his fist under her chin and lifted her face, forcing her to look at him. "I'm thirty-eight-years-old."

Laurel wasn't sure she wanted to hear any of this. The image of his body tangled in a passionate embrace with another woman made her want to cry, to rage, to scream that he belonged to her. "You said you were married once."

"Yeah, for about two days."

"Two days?"

"I was twenty-one and she was eighteen. Her parents had the marriage annulled because they didn't think I was good enough for their precious daughter. She didn't do a damned thing to stop them."

"Did you love her a lot?" Laurel thought how stupid the question sounded. Of course, he would have loved the woman he'd married.

"I worshipped the ground she walked on." He grasped Laurel's chin in his hand when she tried to pull away, shock evident in her eyes.

Laurel knew these memories were painful for him, but she couldn't seem to stop herself from probing deeper. "Did you ever see her again? After the annulment, I mean?"

"Yeah. Once. She called and asked to see me a couple of months later. Stupid kid that I was, I thought she'd changed her mind and was willing to leave her parents," he said in a voice strained with suffering.

"Why did she want to see you if not to reconcile?"

"She thought I had a right to know that she'd had an abortion. Her parents had made other plans for her life that didn't include the baby of some enlisted man with no money and no future." John's face contorted with anguished memories of a woman he'd loved who had betrayed him and destroyed his child.

Laurel realized that he still felt the pain of losing that child, and it hurt to know that she couldn't ease his suffering. Oh, God, she didn't know why the thought of another woman pregnant with his child hurt her so badly, but it did. This man means nothing to you, she reminded herself. Nothing!

"Where is she now?" Laurel wasn't sure why she needed to know what had happened to this girl. But it seemed important somehow.

"She married a young ensign several years later and they've got a couple of kids." John pulled Laurel's face close to his, the warmth of his breath caressing her lips. "There haven't been many women in the last few years. Sex can become pretty routine after a while. I want a lot more from you than sex, Laurel."

"But you want sex from me, don't you?" Of course, he wants sex, you idiot, she told herself. He's a man, a man who wants you as much as you want him.

"If I thought you loved this Carter, I wouldn't stick around hoping something would happen between us. You might find ol' Moody IV socially acceptable, but—"

Laurel pulled away from John. If he weren't touching her, maybe she could think more reasonably. "Carter may be a bit of a snob, but then so am I. I admit it, all right?"

John looked at her and nodded affirmatively but didn't say a word.

"Carter and I share a common background. We want the same things. We understand each other." She knew it was unfair to use Carter as a protective device against John, but she was grasping at straws. She had to have something, someone to shield her from her own unwanted desires.

"Is that enough? What about chemistry? You know, honey, the old butterflies in the stomach. Can he give you the kind of pleasure you deserve?"

Damn him, she thought. I will not let him goad me into admitting that Carter and I have never had a sexual relationship. Mr. Girl-In-Every-Port would get a good laugh if he ever found out just how inexperienced she was. "Carter is one of the finest men I know. He represents everything I admire in a man."

"You've never made love with him, have you?" John ran a hand over his jaw, his fingers rubbing back and forth across his chin. "Stop using him as a wedge between us. There is no one standing between us except you. Be honest."

"I . . . I'm afraid of you and the way you make me feel. There, is that honest enough for you?"

John turned around and reached into the picnic basket and brought out two ripe peaches. He tossed one to Laurel, who was sitting there staring at him as if he had suddenly sprung two heads. She didn't catch the peach. It landed in her lap.

"Dessert," John said when she looked at him questioningly.

Laurel glared down at the peach. She looked quickly to see John's gaze fixed on her untouched fruit. He looked up, and their gazes clashed. He put his peach to his mouth and took a bite. Clear, sweet juice dripped down the corners of his mouth. Laurel swallowed as she watched the descent of the fluid trickle onto his chin. Her hand trembled as she reached down and picked up her peach. She held it in front of her and looked directly into John's black eyes.

He held his peach in one hand and wiped his mouth and chin with the other. "Delicious," he said. "Try yours."

Laurel's hand trembled so badly that she almost dropped the ripe fruit before she reached her mouth. John put one big hand over hers and brought the peach to her lips. She opened her mouth and took a bite, chewing slowly.

John took another bite from his peach, then discarded it. Laurel watched as he took her peach out of her hand. "The only thing I want to taste is you," he said.

As Laurel swallowed the last bite, John threw her fruit away. She quivered with anticipation, afraid to look at him again, knowing that the time for decision had come.

He reached out and ran the tips of his calloused fingers up and down her arm. She groaned, and her body quivered.

"John." His name was a whispered murmur.

"I want to kiss you till you can't breathe," he said, taking her by the shoulders. "I want to taste you, to savor the feel of my mouth on yours."

Laurel closed her eyes, trying to gain some semblance of composure. His look, his words, his nearness were driving her to the brink, to the point of no return.

"I've never wanted another woman the way I want you. It's as if you've crawled inside me, become a part of me."

"I...I..." Could she resist him? she wondered. Did she even want to?

"I want to take off those tiny scraps covering your breasts. I want to look at you, to touch you, to take you into my mouth and love you."

Laurel fell against him as his arms went around her, and he could feel her hardened nipples through her bathing suit, pressing into his chest.

"Tell me it's all right, that you want us to make love," he said, his eyes black and passion-filled as his mouth covered hers in a kiss that blocked out every rational thought from her mind.

Six

John slowly released her swollen mouth. His lips brushed across her jaw and down her neck. Laurel moaned and tossed her head backward while John spread a line of moist kisses on her shoulder and across to the rise of her breast. The humid breeze stirred, bathing her already damp skin with its warmth. The sound of the river, the birds, the wind fingering the greenery echoed in her ears like a distant melody. The world smelled of hot summertime, wilderness air, and John Mason's manly essence.

His mouth covered the tip of her breast, and he suckled her through the thin barrier of her bikini top. Spirals of heat swamped her. She groaned with need and frustration as John moved to the other breast, giving it equal homage. He grasped her waist and pulled her to her knees, his lips sliding to the vulnerable bareness of her stomach. His tongue licked back and forth above her navel, then darted in and out before moving to the edge of her bikini bottoms. Laurel clutched his muscled shoulders. Feverish shudders racked her body.

"I want to hear you say it," he whispered against the taut flesh of her abdomen just before he kissed her there. He fingered the strings of her bikini top. "I want to rip this off you. I don't want anything between my mouth and your breasts. I want to hold them in my hands, to take your nipples in my mouth and suck them until we're both aching for release."

His words formed a hypnotic web around her, catching her in a helpless sensual haze. She wanted him to do all the things he'd said. This was a day apart from the rest of her life, a day she'd enjoy without thought of the consequences. She could make love with John Mason, fulfill the needs of her body that she'd so long denied. But did she dare? Was she capable of such brazen behavior? Was Laurel Drew woman enough to abandon herself to a man without one word of love and forever after?

"John. John, I..." She could feel his breath on her stomach, the pounding of his heart against her flesh.

"If you have any doubts, you'd better say something now, honey, because in a few minutes I won't be able to stop." His hands moved downward, caressing her buttocks, kneading with a slow, easy passion.

Doubt and uncertainty filled her mind and warred with the fury of desire that had her panting for fulfillment. Reason won out for the moment, and she edged backward on the quilt, her knees buckling under her. His arms tightened around her, then reluctantly, he let her go. She could sense his dark gaze covering her like a fierce storm cloud. Feeling certain that he was angry, she couldn't bring herself to face his rage. She trembled, a steady fluttering of nerves that soon shook her whole body with emotions that had no other outlet.

John touched her shoulder. She jerked away, tears filling her violet eyes. "Laurel, it's all right. I'd never do anything to hurt you."

She looked at him, and what she saw made her want to throw herself back into his arms. There was no anger, no fierce rage, only passion and a tenderness so strong that Laurel knew she loved this man, this big wonderful Yankee.

"Oh, John... I do want you. It's just that I don't have a lot of experience, and I've never felt like this before. You frighten me, and I frighten myself."

"I want to make love to you completely," he told her, running his hands up and down the sides of her arms. "But I won't rush you. I'll even let you take charge." There was a mischievous twinkle in his eyes that issued a challenge along with the open invitation.

"I... I'm not sure I understand." Laurel was no longer trembling outside, but her insides felt as if they had been reduced to mush.

John moved away from her and stretched his body out on the quilt. He spread his arms, clutched his hands together, and placed them beneath his head. He closed his eyes and took a deep breath. "I'm all yours, honey. Do whatever you want to do to me. As much or as little as you want. You're in control. You say when we stop."

The realization of what he was offering finally became clear in Laurel's mind. He wanted her to make love to him. "But, John, I don't know how. I've never... never..."

"Look at me, Laurel," he said as he lay there on his back, his eyes still closed. "Look at me. Touch me, and then do whatever feels right."

Laurel wondered if the heat spreading through her body had anything at all to do with the summer sun. Probably not, she thought, since her internal temperature had risen several degrees in mere minutes. She couldn't move or speak, and could barely breathe. Thoughts, images, and ideas flitted through her consciousness like reflections of light off a prism. She took several deep, cleansing breaths, and turned her head.

He's such a big, powerful man, she thought as her eyes moved over his muscular body. John Mason projected an aura of overwhelming strength and total maleness. She moved her gaze quickly over him from the top of his sun-bleached head to the tips of his toes. He didn't move or say a word. He simply lay there, breathing.

His face wasn't really handsome. He lacked the smooth, perfect features to be truly good-looking. But there was a beauty in John's face that came from pure masculinity, features that, taken one at a time, were not remarkable, but put together as a whole, were devastatingly attractive. She remembered the color of his eyes, a brown so dark it appeared black. His cheekbones were high, his jaw square, his nose slightly crooked. His broad mouth curved downward at the edges, accentuating the fullness of his lower lip in contrast to the thin, well-shaped upper. There was only a hint of a dimple in his chin. His ash blond hair was short, but could use a trim, and his rugged face was covered with the stubble of a beard several shades darker than his hair.

With trembling fingers, Laurel reached out and touched John's face, one finger stroking his cheek. She could feel his body tense, then relax. His eyes remained closed, and only the movement of his chest rising and falling told her he was aware of her touch.

All the fingers on that one hand spread out over his face, her thumb caressing his chin. With a whisper-light stroke, she outlined his lips. John opened his mouth slightly, and her finger stroked inside, the tip touching his teeth. John licked her fingertip. Laurel trembled. He took her finger inside his mouth and sucked. He grasped her wrist gently, holding her hand to his lips as, one by one, he lavished identical attention on each of her fingers. Pleasure burned through her body, and Laurel ached with womanly need.

She pulled her hand away, and John's fell back by his side on the quilt.

Unsteady hands touched his massive shoulders as Laurel knelt over him, her eyes devouring the sight of his naked chest. The urge to touch him, to run her fingers over that glorious chest and through the thicket of hair compelled her to act on instinct. Her hands moved slowly, seductively over him, learning every bulge of muscle, every strand of coarse, curly hair, every inch of tanned flesh. She flicked a nail across one tight male nipple and heard John groan deep in his throat. She snatched her hand away, but he grabbed it, kissed her palm, and placed it back on his chest.

"It felt good, honey, so good," he told her as he opened his eyes and looked up at her.

Laurel smiled, feeling more relaxed and more confident. She had never touched a man like this, and she felt a certain heady power, a sense of female strength. The brief affair she'd had with Scott had consisted of quick encounters in the dark, ending with his release and her frustration. She'd been so young, so totally virginal, that she'd had no idea how to be a temptress. She'd never forget that Scott had told her she was a cold, snobby bitch without an ounce of passion in her.

Laurel spread her hands over John's chest, then moved them up and down his arms, squeezing the tight power contained in his muscles. She ran her fingers over the vivid tattoo on his left arm. It wasn't a large tattoo, but it was quite detailed. She traced the shape of the regal bird with her finger, then lowered her head, and acting on pure impulse, followed the same path with the tip of her wet tongue. John's arm hardened to solid stone.

"Lau...rel," he moaned her name as he clenched his hands into tight fists at his side.

"Why...why did you get the tattoo?" She coated the bird with the dampness of her mouth as she kissed his skin.

"I was ... drunk," he mumbled as he struggled for control. He'd promised to let her set the pace, to be totally in charge, but this practically innocent Southern belle was driving him insane. "I was just a ... a kid. I don't remember having it done."

Laurel braced herself on one elbow and looked down at John Mason. She smiled. She'd never known the thrill of controlling a man, and the thought of controlling John affected her like an aphrodisiac. She was hot, her breasts swollen, her nipples pebble-hard, and her body ached with a need to be filled.

"You're a beautiful man, John Mason. The most beautiful man I've ever seen." She lowered her head, running her nose and cheeks across his chest, glorying in the feel of his hair rubbing her skin. She moaned, then buried her face in his chest as her hands moved between them, down to his stomach. Her breasts barely touched him, but her nipples strained for contact. She raised herself slightly, one knee going between his thighs, the other brushing the outside of his leg. Her hands moved across his lower abdomen, her gaze riveted to the tiny black briefs covering the impressive swell of his manhood. She knew he was aroused. The thought was almost as intimidating as the sight. She let her hands separate as they moved over his hips and down the outer curve of his thighs.

"Oh, honey, you're killing me," John looked at her hands as they moved back up his hips and covered his stomach.

"I've never felt so much like a woman in my whole life. You make me want to forget everything and everybody. All I want is to touch you, to be near you, to—"

John grabbed her hands, stopping their exploration, stilling their erotic manipulations. "Don't say things like that unless you intend to back up those words with action."

"I want you to touch me. I want you to—"

He pulled her down on top of him, his hands grasping her hips and rubbing her back and forth against his hardened manhood. "Feel me, honey. Feel how hot and hard I am, how badly I want to be inside you."

"John?" She realized that he'd changed the rules in the middle of the game. She was no longer in charge. He was.

One big hand grabbed her neck, his fingers threading through her long dark hair as he brought her mouth down to his. "Open your mouth," he growled.

Laurel obeyed. He thrust his tongue inside her as he held her head. The kiss went on and on as his hands raked over her, his fingers loosening the tie of her bikini top. He ran his tongue across her bruised lips and down her throat as he jerked the black and lavender material away from her body. Her large, firm breasts fell free, dangling above him like sweet temptation. His mouth covered the tip of one breast while his fingers nipped at the other. Laurel cried out with the pleasurable pain that shot through her.

"Sweet, so sweet." The words were mumbled praise against her flesh.

Laurel felt John's other hand pushing down on her buttocks, seeking closer contact. His mouth moved back and forth from one breast to the other, licking, sucking, stroking until Laurel thought she would explode.

"I want you. I want to be inside you...filling you...giving you all of me."

"Yes. Please love me, Johnny. Please...."

John's body, hard and ready with need, tensed. It doesn't matter what she calls you, he told himself. Even if she thinks I'm her fantasy lover, I'll be the one giving her pleasure. His mouth stilled on her breast as conflicting emotions raged within him. Dammit, it did matter. He didn't want her thinking about anyone except him when he buried himself deep within her. He wanted her to know exactly who he was—John Mason, not Johnny Drew.

John lifted his head and looked at Laurel's flushed face. "Who am I, Laurel? What's my name?"

"What?" She opened her eyes fully and smiled at him. "You're my Johnny," she said dreamily.

John glared at her, hating himself for caring, and hating her for making him want her so. "No, honey, I'm not your Johnny. I'm John Mason, remember?" He pulled away from her, his body trembling with repressed longing.

"I...I... Oh, John, I..." Her breathing was harsh and shallow, her face warm with passion, and her body drugged by desire.

Suddenly they both heard the sound of a speedboat approaching the wharf and the laughter of the people aboard. John reacted quickly, finding her bikini top and helping her put it on. His hands trembled when they touched her heated skin.

The boat stopped and docked, and the passengers called Laurel's name. She heard them through a wild, sensual haze, and her aroused body became rigid. "Oh, Lordy," she cried.

"Who the hell is it?" John asked, his voice a gruff, demanding roar.

Laurel looked down toward the wharf and saw several teenagers. "Oh, mercy, it's Jinn Edwards and some of the Debutantes with their dates."

"It's a damned good thing they didn't show up any sooner or they would have gotten a visual sex-education lesson."

The reality of what she'd almost done hit Laurel, and a mixture of relief and shame filled her heart and mind. How would she ever explain to Jinn and the other girls why she was here at the river with John Mason?

"Trying to figure out a way to explain my presence here, Miss Drew? Why don't you just tell them that I'm here to do some repair work on your boat? You wouldn't be too em-

barrassed if they thought I was your handyman, would
you?''

''John, I—''

He stood up and helped Laurel to her feet, one arm sup-
porting her around the waist. ''This isn't over, honey. We
still have tonight.''

John sat on the edge of the bed in his motel room and
watched Laurel as she stood beside the bed, the telephone
in her hand. During the thirty-five-minute drive from Rose
Trail to Muscle Shoals, John had been able to get himself
under control and put the day's events in the proper perspective. He knew, beyond a shadow of a doubt, that he and
Laurel were destined to become lovers. He'd been a fool to
overreact when she'd called him Johnny. He wouldn't make
that mistake twice. He'd just make damn certain she knew
who was making love to her.

Laurel's little Debutante friends had spent two hours with
them, visiting, swimming, jet skiing, and sharing the re-
mains of their picnic lunch. He knew Laurel had been embarrassed, perhaps a bit ashamed, that the girls had caught
her there with the notorious Yankee stranger. For the life of
him, he couldn't understand Laurel's Southern snobbery.
Of course, he'd never understood Cassie and her parents'
attitude that officers and their families were a breed apart
from enlisted men. But that was the past, and he had no intention of allowing the insecurities he'd felt then to interfere with his desire for Laurel.

As he watched her now, he could hardly believe she'd so
readily agreed to come back with him to his motel room.
The atmosphere between them had definitely cooled before
they left the river, and neither had said much of anything on
their trip up Highway 72. Right before they'd reached the
turnoff for the DuBois-Drew Home, John asked her to go
back into town with him. He'd even offered to let her stop
and change clothes, and had been surprised when she'd put

her hand on his leg and said, "I thought you said we still have tonight."

"Aunt Polly," Laurel said into the phone. "Hi. I'm not going to be home until later. John and I are going out for supper."

"What are you going to wear?" Polly asked.

"The skirt and blouse I wore over my bathing suit."

"Well, I guess that will be suitable if you aren't planning on going anywhere fancy."

Laurel laughed, realizing that even a freethinker like Aunt Polly drew the line at being inappropriately dressed. "Did Bonnie Jean call about the Friends of the Library meeting this Sunday?"

"No. I haven't heard a word from her, but Laurel, I do have something to tell you."

"What?"

"You might not want to say anything to John about it until we have a chance to speak privately about this later."

"What are you talking about?"

"I went through Clarice's old trunk again."

"Why? We've been through it a couple of times already." Laurel smiled across the bed at John who blew her a kiss.

"I found something in the secret compartment," Aunt Polly said.

"That's impossible. I found that secret compartment years ago and it was empty." Laurel watched John raise his eyebrows questioningly and wondered why she felt a sudden sense of apprehension.

"Oh," Aunt Polly said, then became unnaturally silent.

"Aunt Polly, what's this all about?"

"There's something I have to show you, something very important, but it can wait until tomorrow. You and John have a wonderful night. And don't bother getting home early. As a matter of fact . . ." The old woman let her sentence trail off into silence.

"As a matter of fact, what?"

"Nothing. Just have a good time. And take a chance."

Before Laurel could reply, her aunt hung up, and the humming telephone indicated their conversation had ended.

Laurel put the receiver down and turned to John. "I think my very moral great-aunt just gave me permission to spend the night with you."

"Aunt Polly likes me," he said, patting the bed, inviting her to join him. "She thinks I'm destined to be your Yankee lover."

"I can't spend the night," Laurel said, wondering who would know and who would tell if she did allow herself that one special indulgence.

"How long have you lived with your aunt?" John patted the bed again, and she sat down.

"Actually, I don't live with Aunt Polly. I've been spending the summer out there taking advantage of all the Du Bois-Drew papers and books in the old library." Laurel ran her fingertips beneath his shirt, teasing his nipples.

"You're playing with fire, little girl. You could get burned."

Laurel withdrew her hand, then slowly, almost methodically, unbuttoned his shirt and spread it away from his chest. "Would you believe I still live at home with my parents?"

"You aren't serious?" He pulled her down on top of him, his lips nuzzling at her neck.

"Aunt Polly found . . . oh, John, stop that."

"Aunt Polly found what?" he asked, his mouth seeking hers while his hands clutched her hips.

Laurel kissed him quickly, pulling her head upward and away from his. "She said she found something in the secret compartment of Grandmother Clarice's old trunk."

"Let's talk about old trunks later." His lips captured hers, and she responded by melting into him, her arms resting on each side of his head as she helped him deepen the kiss.

Half-drugged by the heady sensations the kiss evoked within her, Laurel lay her head in the curve of his neck and nipped tiny love-bites from his earlobe to his shoulder. "Aunt Polly said she had something very important to show me. It could be something about Johnny Drew," she whispered.

One big hand caressed the back of her head, his fingers tangling in the black mass of her hair while his other hand rubbed rhythmically up and down her back. "If this information has been a secret for over a hundred years, one more night won't make any difference," John said as his stroking hand lowered to the waistband of her skirt and tugged on the drawstring holding the material together.

"What happened to that shower you were going to take?" Laurel asked teasingly.

"Oh, I still intend to take a shower. I was just waiting for you to agree to join me." His hand in her hair circled her neck and brought her head downward where his mouth found her throat, his tongue covering her skin with moist warmth.

Laurel's low, feverish moan mixed with the sound of John's masculine groan. "I...we..." Laurel stumbled over her words, trying to tell him that he was moving too fast for her. "I thought we had plans to go out for supper."

"Tonight, I have other plans."

"Oh, and just what might those other plans be?" Laurel pulled away from him and got up off the bed.

"I thought that this high school history teacher I know might be interested in giving me some private lessons." He moved off the bed quickly, his dark eyes sparkling with devilment.

He stood a couple of feet away from her, his shirt unbuttoned all the way down the front, revealing his incredibly sexy chest. His jeans were skin tight, accentuating the hard leanness of his body, the firm masculine muscles.

"I don't usually give private lessons to ex-sailors with eagles tattooed on their arms."

"Would you consider making an exception in my case?" he asked as he took a step closer. "My credentials are the best."

Laurel's heartbeat drummed in her ears. She wanted him to take that last step, to reach out and take her in his arms, and kiss her until they were both wild with desire. "Just what are your credentials?" Laurel took a deep breath, then closed the gap between them as she stepped forward and put her arms around his neck.

John grabbed her around the waist and hauled her up against him. "I'm your Yankee lover come to fulfill your fantasies."

Oh, God, why had he said that? Laurel's mind screamed. Because he knew it was the one thing you wanted to hear, she told herself. Because in both your hearts, you know that's exactly what he is—your Yankee lover.

"Sir, I do believe your credentials are impeccable," she sighed just as his lips brushed across hers, their breaths mingling.

He kissed her tenderly, with the restraint of a gentleman courting his lady. But the hands that roamed up and down her back, finally delving beneath the waistband of her skirt, didn't belong to a gentleman. He pulled on her skirt until it loosened and fell to her feet in a lavender puddle. Laurel stepped out of it and kicked it aside. She pulled on John's shirt until she maneuvered his arms out of it.

"You, sir, smell like the river." She threw his shirt on the floor beside her skirt."

"Is that a hint for me to take a bath?" John untied the strings of the bikini top, hands roaming over her shoulder blades.

"Don't you think I smell like the river, too?" she asked while her fingers fumbled with the snap of his jeans.

"I definitely think a shower is in order for both of us."
Just as Laurel unsnapped his jeans, John ran his hand between them and removed her bikini top.

"Are you inviting me to take one with you?" Laurel
asked while she unzipped his jeans.

A shudder racked his body. The feel of Laurel's fingers
so near his manhood almost sent him out of control. "I'm
inviting you to bathe me and let me bathe you."

Together they slipped his jeans down his legs. When he
reached out to pull her back into his arms, she moved away
from him, her bare breasts tempting him beyond reason.
"Laurel?"

"Go get the water good and hot," she laughed, dodging
his grasp as he moved closer.

"You're playing games, lady." John growled as he
grabbed her, pulling her against him as his lips found hers.

This is right, Laurel thought, so right. She wanted to be
with John, to become his lover. She knew the only thing that
should matter was the here and now, this moment and the
beautiful moments that could follow. What she'd felt for
Scott had been a college crush on a football hero. He'd been
an insensitive jerk whose condemning appraisal of her as a
woman and lover still haunted her. But this man wasn't
Scott. He was John Mason—her Yankee lover. And this
wild, uncontrollable yearning within her was love, passionate love.

John held her fiercely against him, his arousal hot and
hard, as his mouth continued to ravage hers.

You can do this, she told herself. You want to go with
him, to feel his hands on your body. You want to touch him
and kiss him and learn every muscled inch of him. But what
if she failed him? What if she weren't woman enough to
please him? John was a man with vast experience, and he
would expect her to... Oh, dear Lord, she couldn't do this.
She couldn't chance making a fool of herself with a man
who could destroy her pride and break her heart.

"John, I . . ." Laurel pulled out of his arms. "I want you to go on in and start the shower. Okay?"

"Laurel, honey, what's wrong?" He took a tentative step toward her but stopped when he saw the unmistakable fear in her eyes. The last thing he ever wanted was for her to be afraid of him.

"I...uh...I'm not quite ready for this. I mean...I need a few minutes alone."

"Okay. I'll get the water good and warm." John reached out and pulled her limp hand into his and tugged her forward. He put her hand to his lips, kissed her palm tenderly, and looked into her frightened eyes. "I'll be waiting for you whenever you're ready."

"Yes," she gulped the word, relief spreading through her as he turned toward the bathroom. "Thank you."

John stopped in the doorway, his back still facing her. "I'll never hurt you, honey, and that's a promise."

Seven

——

John pulled back the curtain and adjusted the water for the intimate shower he visualized in his mind. He stripped off his swim briefs and stepped beneath the warm water. He waited, expecting Laurel to join him at any moment.

He knew she was skittish about bathing with him, but knew she wanted him as desperately as he wanted her. He'd understood that she needed a few minutes alone in which to build up her courage. She'd probably never done something like this before in her life, and he didn't want to push her too hard or too fast.

John stood beneath the warm water, wondering how long she was going to keep him waiting. Finally he stuck his head out from under the refreshing spray and listened. He didn't hear a sound.

"Laurel?"

No reply came from the other room. Just what the hell's going on, he wondered as he stepped out of the shower and reached for a towel. "Laurel, honey, what's taking you so long?"

When she didn't answer, he draped the white towel around his hips and walked into the adjoining room. Laurel stood beside the bed dressed in her gauzy lavender skirt and blouse. She looked up at him, her eyes glazed, her face pale.

"Honey, what's wrong?" John took several steps toward her, fear gripping him.

"I can't," she whimpered. "I want to, but I can't."

John's dark eyes widened in surprise. Dear God, no, he thought. Who had done this to her? Who had made her so afraid of loving?

Laurel slumped down on the side of the bed, tears filling her eyes. "I'm sorry."

John eased down beside her, letting his clasped hands hang loosely between his legs. "It's all right, Laurel." He wanted to touch her but didn't dare. "Do you want to tell me about it?"

"I don't know if I can." She crossed her arms over her breasts and grabbed her shoulders, her whole body trembling.

"I'm a good listener." He didn't move a fraction even though he wanted, more than anything, to take her in his arms and hold her.

"I was very popular in high school. I was president of my social club, head cheerleader, homecoming queen." She didn't look at John.

"I can see why. You were probably as beautiful a girl as you are a woman." John's gaze covered her slowly from head to toe, his dark eyes finding a pleasure his hands longed to enjoy.

"That was only part of it. Being a Drew helped, believe me. But the point I'm trying to make is that here in my own hometown, I knew only a certain kind of life, a certain kind of people. My parents and community pretty well dictated what I did, who I dated, and what was expected of me.''

''You're trying to tell me that you led a fairly sheltered life, right?''

''Until I went away to college.'' The memories rushed in on her, attacking her from every corner of her mind. ''My senior year, I met a boy named Scott Baker. He was a football player attending college on an athletic scholarship. He was good-looking, exciting, and every girl on campus was after him. But he wanted me. Or, at least, I thought he did.''

John knew she was on the verge of tears, that even though she was determined to purge her soul, she wasn't really prepared to reopen old wounds. ''I don't have to know this, Laurel. I don't care about your past.''

She placed her hands, palms down, on each side of her. ''If we... I have to... Scott was the first and only man I've ever... ever... been with.''

At first John thought he'd misunderstood what she'd said. Did ''been with'' mean had sex with? he wondered. My God, had a woman as beautiful and desirable as Laurel had only one lover? ''Are you saying that... that...''

''Scott was my only lover.'' Feelings of shame and self-loathing came back to her as if the events had occurred only yesterday instead of nine years ago.

John wanted this guy Scott dead. It was obvious that he'd hurt Laurel terribly, that even now she couldn't remember him and the time they'd shared without renewed suffering.

John turned to her, and the agony he saw on her face brought out every loving and protective instinct within him. ''Tell me, honey. Tell me, and then let it go forever.''

Laurel felt the trembling begin in her hands, then move to her arms and shoulders. A slow, consuming ache started in her chest, expanding until it almost choked her. ''He was different from any boy I'd ever dated. He was the opposite of my father, brother, and uncles. He was a little bit like you, John. Rugged, rough, and so very, very manly.''

The comparison between himself and the monster who'd hurt Laurel filled him with pain as if he had caused some of her anguish himself. He knew one thing for certain—he hated Scott Baker enough to hope for Scott's sake they never met. "He was no Southern gentleman, I take it," John said, wanting desperately to hold her in his arms and comfort her.

"Oh, he was Southern all right. A good ol' boy. Sex was a pastime for him, and girls were just part of the game." The trembling within her grew until the signs were outwardly visible. She swayed toward John, and he took her into his arms. "Scott saw me as a challenge because...because I was beautiful...and...and came from a socially prominent family."

"Go on, honey, finish it." John felt her body racked with mental and emotional pain, and the only thing he could do was stroke her and encourage her to get it all out.

She held back the tears burning her throat and clouding her eyes. "He went after me determined to make me fall in love with him. He brought out all the sexual feelings I'd kept buried because I'd been taught to save my virginity for the man I married. But Scott told me he loved me, that he wanted marriage someday. Fool that I was, I believed him. I didn't know. I didn't know." She cried then, hard and cleansing.

John held her so tightly, so fiercely that he was afraid he might hurt her, but he knew she needed his strength. "That's it, honey."

Sobbing, Laurel mumbled, incoherently at first, and then a few words at a time. "A bet...he made...love to me...to win a bet. Some of his buddies...ones I said no to. He bet them he could get me in his bed and keep me there as long as he wanted me."

John held her, absorbing her pain, the very intensity nearly ripping him apart. "Go ahead and cry. Get it all out and put it behind you. I promise that no one will ever hurt you again."

"We were...lovers...for about six weeks before I found out. I went to his apartment and found him with another girl. He was telling her about me. They were...laughing. Then he said...he said he was glad I'd found out because he was tired of fooling with...with...a frigid little snob who didn't know the first thing about pleasing a man."

Dear Lord, Laurel thought, how can it still hurt like this? "Oh, John, don't you understand? I can't ever risk going through something like that again." She pulled away from him slightly, her hands clutching his forearms.

"Don't do this to yourself, Laurel. You've spent years punishing yourself for something that wasn't your fault."

"I should have known better," she sobbed. "He wasn't my kind. My parents had warned me."

John ran the back of his hand under her chin, encouraging her to look at him. "Scott Baker was a damned fool!"

"I want you, John—more than I ever wanted Scott—but I'm so afraid."

"My feelings for you are real. I'd never ever hurt you."

"But you've already hurt me without meaning to. You came into my life and awakened emotions I thought had died. You made me feel desire for a man totally unsuitable for me. And then you...you confronted me with all those accusations about Pappy Drew."

"Give me a chance, Laurel. Give me a chance to prove myself to you."

"But...what if I disappoint you?"

"Oh, honey." Her self-doubts broke his heart. This lovely, insecure woman brought out a possessive streak in him he'd never known existed. She also exposed a tender, vulnerable side of his nature that scared the hell out of him. He wasn't the type of man for commitment, but Laurel Drew had him thinking about their tomorrows. "What if I disappoint you?"

"What?" Her big, violet eyes opened wide as she searched his face for humor. What she saw was a depth of

emotions glowing in his eyes and loving care written plainly
on his manly features.

John took her hand in his and helped her to her feet. Her
knees threatened to buckle when she stood, but he braced
her trembling body against his side. "Let me love you,
Laurel. Let me try to please you."

"Oh...." Her heart beat savagely within her chest, the
roar in her ears blocking out every other sound.

"Let me prove to you how much of a woman you really
are." John tugged on her hand and led her toward the
bathroom.

As they stood in the bathroom doorway, Laurel could
hear the water still running in the shower. For the first time,
she really looked at John and realized he was naked except
for a small white towel draped around his waist.

John felt her hesitation and saw her staring at him. "Slow
and easy," he said. "Just follow my lead, sweetheart. All I
want to do is give you pleasure."

Fear and desire warred within Laurel as she stood on the
threshold of the unknown. Did she dare trust John Mason?
Did she dare trust her own judgment? She knew she was
falling in love with John, and if she gave herself to him, she
might want more from him than he could give.

"I want you. I..." She'd take tonight and let tomorrow
take care of itself. Even if the only commitment between
them was in her heart, it didn't matter.

Step-by-step, John led her into the bathroom and to the
shower. He pulled back the curtain, and Laurel could feel
the warm spray hitting her arm. He stepped into the shower
and drew Laurel, fully clothed, inside with him. He removed the towel from his waist, tossed it onto the floor, and
closed the shower curtain.

Laurel forced herself not to look down. She knew he was
totally naked while she was completely covered. The very
thought sent a wildness coursing through her. The warm

water drenched her within a few seconds, her thin skirt and blouse clinging to her like damp gauze.

John let his eyes travel slowly from the top of Laurel's wet hair, its natural curl creating a cascade of black silk, to the tips of her bare feet. He knew that tonight would be a monumental test of his ability to control his baser instincts. But his own needs had to be secondary to Laurel's. Her pleasure would be his.

His fingers clasped the top button of her wet blouse. When he opened that first button, he heard a tiny gasp escape from her lips. With each button, he moved the tip of his finger down Laurel's chest, between her breasts, and over her stomach to the waistband of her skirt. He eased the soaking material from her shoulders and let it fall to her feet.

Laurel began to tingle inside, as if some alien force had entered her body. She felt as if she should do something, move, or talk, or reach out and touch him, but she couldn't. She simply stood there, with the warm water caressing her, and let John run his fingers through her hair, clasp her head and pull her face toward his. His lips covered her damp face with a series of light kisses, and his tongue outlined the bone structure from cheekbone to chin.

Laurel whimpered and leaned into him when his mouth covered hers, his tongue thrusting inside. His big hands released her head, slid down her back, and clutched her hips. He pulled her against his arousal. Laurel cried out and grabbed his bare shoulders.

John deepened the kiss, consuming her with a raging desire he fought to control. He knew he was allowing things to get out of hand, but he needed just one more kiss before he could stop. He took that kiss while Laurel clung to him, her body pressed into his while he fondled her lovingly.

When Laurel whimpered again, John dropped his hands from her hips and grabbed her by the waist, putting a few inches between their wet bodies. "Let's get you out of that skirt, honey." The depth and virility of his voice filled the small shower cubicle and surrounded Laurel like a caressing hand.

He pulled at her skirt until he'd loosened it. When she tried to help him, he pushed her shaky hands aside and slowly eased the skirt down her hips. He bent on one knee in front of her, and with both hands, drew the lavender material down her thighs and calves. When the skirt fell to her ankles, John lowered his mouth and hands to her legs. His hands moved over the sides of her thighs, caressing, massaging, exploring. His mouth touched the front of her thighs, and Laurel felt the contact in every nerve of her body. When his tongue drew a line along the inside of her leg, she cried out and begged him to stop.

John looked up at her. Her head was tossed back, her neck arched, and her hands gripped his shoulders. As the warm shower water poured down on her face, she shook with desire. John ran his hands up and down her legs from hips to ankles and back again before standing up and taking her in his arms.

He had never wanted to make love to a woman as badly as he did Laurel. And he had never wanted more to give a woman pleasure. The intensity of his feelings for this woman frightened him. It was as if he'd been waiting his entire life to find her—as if he'd been born to love her.

Laurel responded to his kisses with a passion that should have surprised her, but didn't. John Mason brought out every primeval, sexual element in her nature. With him she was woman—soft and giving, wild with abandon, and open to his predatory claim. And he was man—hard and commanding, savagely tender, and demanding sole possession.

When John tugged on the straps of her bikini top, Laurel ran her hands across his broad back. He untied the strings securing the skimpy material together while his tongue and teeth took turns lavishing attention on Laurel's neck and shoulder. He dropped the wet bikini and moved his hands between them, cupping her breasts. She let her body go limp, her arms falling to her sides. Then he touched the tip of one breast with his finger and thumb, squeezing gently. Laurel opened her eyes and looked down just in time to see his head lower to the other breast. The sight of him suckling her jolted her like a lightning bolt.

"Oh, John...Johnny!" she cried out, her body aching for the fulfillment only he could give her.

"Slow and easy," he mumbled against her breast. "We have all the time in the world."

"I don't know how much more I can take," she told him and pulled at his head, trying to stop his marauding mouth from sending her over the edge.

John kissed both her breasts, then kissed a trail up her chest and neck, to her chin, and finally her mouth. Laurel shoved him backward and held both hands up in front of her. "Make love to me, Johnny. Please make love to me."

"That's what I'm doing, my sweet Southern belle," he said.

Laurel looked at him then, her eyes moving over him slowly. He didn't make a move to take her back in his arms or to touch her. He allowed her all the time she needed to devour every inch of him, savoring the sight of his nakedness. She'd never known a man could be so beautiful, so big, and completely male. Hesitantly, timidly, she reached out and touched him, encompassed his maleness within her hand. John's whole body tensed, and he emitted a groan from deep within his chest.

Quickly, surely, he slipped her bikini briefs down her legs, his hand delving for that secret womanly spot between her thighs, seeking and finding. Laurel shook when he touched her and cried out his name over and over, "Johnny...Johnny...."

And while he loved her with his fingers, the warm water covered them, heating their feverish bodies. Laurel had never known anything like the sensations his capable fingers gave her. When she trembled with the force of her release and clung to him, crying, pleading, thanking, he lifted her to him. She tightened her legs around his hips as he held her securely in his arms and thrust into her with a wildness that no amount of reason could have tamed.

He held her hips, moving them back and forth until he couldn't take anymore. The tremors of his body detonated her already sensitive nerve endings, sending her into an intense release. He pressed her against the back of the shower stall, and ever so slowly, let her slide downward, her slick, tingling flesh clinging to his.

He held her in his arms, his lips running rampant over her face as he praised her lovingly. "Laurel, my beautiful, beautiful mermaid. You were perfect. We were perfect together."

"Oh, Johnny, we were, weren't we?" This was the way it was meant to be between a man and a woman—this giving and taking—this unbearable pleasure.

John took a draw on his cigarette, inhaling deeply, as he watched Laurel put on her damp skirt and blouse. Even though they had spent the last several hours giving each other exquisite pleasure, she was running scared. She knew it, and so did he. It made him mad as hell, and he'd told her so. Then he'd practically begged her to stay the night, and finally, after she'd made it perfectly clear that she intended to go home, he'd agreed to drive her.

"This has been the most wonderful night of my life," she told him as she bent down to slip on her sandles. "But this isn't some big city where nobody cares what their neighbors do. I know you think I'm being foolish, but I do have a reputation to uphold and so does my family. Please try to understand."

"Oh, I understand," John said. "I just don't happen to agree with you."

"I wanted you. Heaven help me, I still want you." Laurel stood up straight and looked at him, her heart catching in her throat at the mere sight of his naked chest as he sat on the bed in nothing but his jeans.

"Yeah, I know. You've already said it. You want me, but there's too many differences in our life-styles, too many unanswered questions about ol' Johnny Drew for us to continue our affair. Does that about cover it?" Dammit all, he wanted to shake some sense into that beautiful head. As far as he was concerned, the only thing standing between them was her stubborn pride—her genteel Southern arrogance!

"You've given me so much tonight, made me feel—"

"Save it, huh? Don't tell me what a damned good lover I am one minute and then the next tell me I'm not good enough for you."

"Oh, John, I never said such a thing. And I never said that we can't be...friends...maybe even more... eventually."

"When?" He stood up, reached down on the bed for his shirt, and slipped it on.

"When we're both sure we know what we want from this relationship."

"After what we shared tonight, I thought that should be obvious."

"As long as I live, I'll never regret tonight, but I'm not a woman who can handle temporary love affairs. I want and need more."

"And you think I'm not capable of something permanent?"

"Tonight is not the time for either of us to make rash promises. I need some time, and so do you."

"I don't need anything but you, honey." He reached out and took her by the shoulders.

"Please take me home." She looked at him with such pleading in her soft violet eyes that John's anger melted.

"You're the most stubborn woman I've ever known."

Eight

Laurel stood looking out the window, her eyes seeing none of the summer beauty of the well-kept grounds surrounding the DuBois-Drew Home. She'd spent a restless night thinking about John Mason and what had happened between them. She had no doubts about her feelings. She was madly, passionately in love with the flesh and blood version of her fantasy Yankee lover. For the first time in her life she understood the extent of her ancestors' love for each other. If Clarice DuBois had loved her Johnny with such mindless desire, then she would have accepted him regardless of his past.

But am I that brave? Laurel wondered. Can I go against everything I've treasured all my life in order to have an affair with John Mason? If only he could promise her total commitment. Then she might be able to reconcile the emotions warring within her.

The only time in her life she'd gone against her proper upbringing, she'd paid dearly. Only John's lovemaking last night had ended the guilt and shame she'd felt for so long. Her feelings for Scott Baker had been nothing compared to the way she loved John. He had the power to destroy not only her dream of publishing Johnny Drew's biography, but her very life.

Why couldn't she have fallen in love with Carter or someone as equally suitable? John wasn't a gentleman. He wasn't cultured or college educated. He'd learned all about life the hard way—by living it. He wanted to spend that life in St. Augustine as a partner in his friend Nate's boating business. His lack of ambition would appall her father, and his roughneck manners would shock her mother.

"Laurel?" Polly Drew entered the back parlor, clutching a small leather journal in her hands. "I really must speak with you, dear."

"Oh, Aunt Polly, please come in."

"Forgive me for interrupting your solitude, but this can't wait any longer." Polly closed the connecting doors leading into the gentlemen's parlor.

"What is it?" Laurel faced her aunt whose complexion was deathly pale.

"It's about Grandmother Clarice's trunk," Polly whispered as if she thought the walls were listening. She held out the leather-bound book to Laurel. "It's Clarice DuBois's personal diary. It was in the secret compartment of the trunk."

"Oh, Aunt Polly, this is wonderful." Laurel reached out and grabbed the diary, ignoring the stricken look on her great-aunt's face.

"Laurel, don't you think it odd that I should have discovered the diary now?" Polly put special emphasis on the word "now."

Laurel understood immediately that her aunt meant now that John Mason was in Tuscumbia claiming Johnny Drew was a bigamist. "This diary wasn't in the secret compart-

ment, was it? You and I have searched that trunk a dozen
times, and I know the secret compartment was empty."

"It was every time you searched through it."

"Then where . . . how can—"

"I've always known the diary was in the secret compartment. Your Uncle William told me. When . . . when you decided to go through the trunk for research material for your
book, I removed the diary."

Laurel's hands trembled as she looked down at the journal. "Why?"

"Forgive me, my dear, but . . . well, the things in this
journal were family secrets. They would have ended your
dreams."

"I see." Laurel felt a chill run through her as if an icy
hand had touched her bare skin. "Is there any mention
of . . . of . . ." She couldn't bring herself to ask the question
tormenting her mind.

"You may want to be alone when you read it." Polly's
gaze rested on Laurel's trembling hands, then moved
pleadingly to her niece's stricken face. "I've read it, my
dear, and there are things . . . well, very personal things."

John stood beside his parked Jag, lit a cigarette, and
stared at the veranda of the DuBois-Drew Home. He'd
come here uninvited and probably unwelcome, but he was
determined to see Laurel and straighten out things once and
for all. He'd spent the whole night trying to come to terms
with what had happened after their tempestuous lovemaking. Laurel wanted him. He was damned sure about that,
but she was ashamed of him. And that hurt his masculine
pride. No man wanted his woman to be ashamed of him.

The logical part of his brain told him to cut his losses, to
forget Laurel Drew, and go to Florida. His heart told him
that he wanted Laurel enough to stay and help her overcome her fears and uncertainties.

Instead of getting a few hours sleep last night, he'd lain awake visualizing the passionate woman he'd brought to life during hours of hot and steamy loving. All he could see, all he could think about was a black-haired witch with a Southern drawl and an incredible body.

John took one last draw on his cigarette and dropped it onto the gravel drive. He reached into the car and picked up the small tintype of J. T. Andrews and his Ohio bride on their wedding day. He'd had the thing packed away in his suitcase, waiting for the right moment to show it to Laurel. The right moment had never come. Until now. Now, when he needed an excuse to see her.

He wasn't sure what he'd say once he got her alone. The truth, the whole truth was probably the only thing that would save him, the only thing that would convince Laurel to give their relationship a chance. He'd realized sometime early this morning that he loved Laurel. He loved her more than he'd ever loved anyone or anything in his life. It was the kind of illogical, unreasonable, and unexplainable kind of emotion that overruled common sense. It came from a place so deep inside a man that until he'd loved like this, he didn't even know the feelings existed.

It was sex. Sure it was. Just the thought of making love to Laurel aroused him. He'd been walking around most of the morning with the physical proof. But sex was only part of it. There was a tenderness, a possessiveness, and a need to care for and protect in these wild new emotions that could be nothing else but love. Real, honest-to-God love. For the first time in his life, he was really in love with a woman, and half the time she was ashamed of him, and the other half of the time she had him confused with some fantasy lover from the pages of history.

Clutching the picture in his hand, John walked toward the veranda. He knew he'd have to deal with more than Laurel's fears when he walked through the front door of the old mansion. That is, if he made it through the front door. Not even Aunt Polly's whispered encouragement over the phone earlier this morning had eased his uncertainties.

John noticed the front door standing slightly ajar as he neared the entrance. Odd, he thought. Had Aunt Polly left the front door unlocked for him? He pushed the huge door open and stepped inside, feeling a momentary guilt at not announcing himself properly. What the hell, Laurel was already convinced he wasn't a gentleman.

Deciding his best bet was to find Aunt Polly first, John moved down the central hallway and past the front parlor. As he drew closer to the back parlor, he heard voices. Laurel's and Aunt Polly's. John moved to the double doors leading into the room and stationed himself beside the wall near the opening. He peered inside where he saw Laurel clutching a small leather journal to her breast.

"Your Grandmother mentions J. T. Andrews," Polly announced, pointing to the diary. "Look toward the end of her journal. It's something she wrote in her old age after Johnny Drew was dead."

John tensed, and he gripped the picture in his hand so tightly that the ancient glass covering cracked under pressure. As indecision soared through his mind, he lay the tintype on the trestle table behind him. He drew in several deep breaths. Damn! He knew he should walk into the room and let Laurel know that he was here. But he didn't. He couldn't.

Ignoring her aunt's concern, Laurel walked across the parlor and sat down in the Chippendale chair near the window. Tentatively and with great reverence, she opened her great-great-grandmother's diary. The pages were worn and yellow with age. Clarice's handwriting was large and precise, showing her tutelage in penmanship.

Fear and excitement warred within Laurel for a dominant position. Aunt Polly had as good as said that John Mason's accusations were true, but she had to read her ancestress's words before she would believe it. She turned the pages slowly, silently, praying that the dreams and fantasies of her youth would not all be destroyed. Please, Lord, she begged, let Johnny Drew have been half the man I thought he was.

"Laurel?" Polly whispered her name when she stood beside the chair and placed her hand on the younger woman's shoulder. "You can make the necessary changes in the biography. You're so close to finishing the book, you can't let this stop you."

"All I lack is the final chapter and some revisions."

Laurel couldn't imagine changing the image of a man whose memory was honored by the entire county. "I won't write anything that will change people's opinions of Johnny Drew."

John knew he couldn't stand there hiding behind the door any longer. What she was about to read was going to hurt Laurel deeply, but the truth just might free her from the chains that kept her bound to a life he could never be a part of.

He walked into the room from the hallway. "Why don't you read the diary out loud so we can both hear."

Laurel gasped as she looked at John, shock and hurt apparent in the misty gleam of her violet eyes. "I...I..."

"Go ahead, honey, read Clarice's diary so we can find out the truth." John stepped farther into the parlor.

"You were eavesdropping!" Laurel cried, clutching the diary tightly. "How dare you come into this house uninvited and unannounced."

"The front door was open." This visit wasn't turning out anything like he'd planned. He hadn't counted on Aunt Polly's revelation about the hidden diary turning into a nightmare that would ruin Laurel's dream biography and possibly make her hate him for instigating the inquiry into J. T. Andrews's past.

"You're not welcome here." Laurel's eyes darkened to blue-black as she fought the onslaught of tears threatening to erupt at any moment.

"I'm not leaving until I hear the truth from Clarice DuBois. I think you'd agree that I have as much right to know the truth as you do." He knew he was pushing her, but dammit, nothing could be solved between them until she faced some hard truths about dear ol' Pappy Drew.

"Stay," Laurel said. "Stay and listen. Then I want you to get out of this house and out of this town and never come back."

A nervous quiet filled the parlor as two people waited for Laurel to reopen the diary and read. Laurel closed her eyes, blinking back tears, cursing herself for being secretly thankful that John was here to share the secrets of the past. She opened her eyes and slowly turned the pages of the diary. She flipped through the aged sheets toward the final entries, skimming whole paragraphs as she read. Suddenly she sucked in her breath. Her hands trembled as she began to read aloud.

Today is my wedding anniversary. If Johnny were alive, we would be celebrating fifty-five years of wedded bliss. But I cannot complain, for we had a lifetime of love and passion, and we leave three fine sons to carry on in our stead. It is to and for these sons that I write these words. I feel you, my children, have a right to know the truth about your father and me, and the depth of our love and commitment to each other.

As rumor goes, your father was a wounded Union officer whom I nursed back to health, and he has been revered as a patriot of the Southern cause. My Johnny was indeed a deserter, but never a traitor, because his devotion was to our cause and not that of the Union. He left the army because of me, and because of me, he could never return to Ohio, to his family, and the life he had once known.

Johnny had an older brother who died shortly before Johnny enlisted in the army. This brother left his young fiancée with child, and it was decided by Johnny's family that he should marry the girl. As a matter of family honor, he married a woman he didn't love. When he joined the army, he left his young bride behind, never dreaming that while fighting for his country on enemy soil, he would fall in love with a stranger. Because of the war and circumstances, Johnny and I decided to change his name from John Terrence Andrews to Johnny Drew. For all intents and purposes, he deserted the Union army and worked for the Confederate cause. My father reported Johnny's death to his commanding officer who was responsible for notifying the family.

If our choices hurt anyone, they hurt Johnny the most because he never saw his parents or brothers and sisters again. If I had it to do over, I would, for I loved Johnny Drew with all my heart and soul, as he did me.

Laurel sat immobile, a thin trail of tears streaming down her face, and she clung to the diary as if it were a lifeline.

Polly Drew stepped around the chair to stand in front of Laurel. She reached out and touched her niece's trembling hands. "Your great-great-grandfather was a good man, Laurel, and any wrongs he committed were for good reasons. You can write the truth about him without any shame."

"How...how...can you...say that?" Laurel gulped the words as she continued crying. "He was a...a bigamist. He already had a wife when he married Grandmother Clarice."

"So, my great-grandmother was the child born to J. T. Andrews's Ohio wife," John said, feeling a sense of relief that ol' Johnny Drew wasn't quite the black-hearted villain he'd assumed.

"Aunt Polly would never have... have given me this diary if you hadn't..." Laurel said, loosening her hold on the diary with one hand so she could wipe the tears from her cheeks. "This... this damned diary would have stayed hidden forever!" Laurel threw the journal to the floor and buried her face in her hands.

Instinctively John moved toward Laurel, the protective, possessive love he felt for her demanding that he ease her pain. But before John could reach Laurel, Aunt Polly stepped between them. She shook her head and gave him a warning look, then stepped aside. Polly knelt, retrieved the diary, and walked silently out of the room.

It's true, Laurel thought. Pappy Drew was a bigamist. Clarice was never legally his wife. Not ever. And their three sons were illegitimate. How can I possibly finish the biography now? It would mean either lying or exposing my whole family to the sordid truth. What would people think?

Laurel wiped the tears from her eyes and tried to focus her attention on John Mason. "I'd... I'd like to ask you for a solemn promise."

He wanted to touch her, to enfold her in his arms and kiss away the pain. But he couldn't. She would never allow it, this genteel Southern lady.

Laurel forced herself to look at John. The smug assurance she'd expected to see on his face was not there. His black eyes bored into hers, their expression one of care and concern. She didn't want to see such emotion, such genuine feelings coming from a man whose message from the past had ruined her future.

"No one will ever hear any of this from me. As far as I'm concerned, Johnny Drew's memory can continue in sainthood."

She closed her eyes, shutting out the sight of the man she loved, hoping to ease the pain rooted so deeply within her heart.

Laurel sighed. "What I want from you is a promise that you will never repeat anything that's been discussed here today. That you'll never tell anyone that Johnny Drew was actually J. T. Andrews."

John touched Laurel's arm, his fingers moving down to clasp her wrist. "Do you even need to ask for my promise?" he whispered, stroking the inside of her wrist with his thumb.

A sensation of pure female response spread through her body, like the dawn light slowly awakening the earth. In her heart, she loved John Mason and trusted him, but did she dare believe her heart? Her body agreed with her heart's decision, but her mind still struggled with doubts and confusion.

Laurel bit her bottom lip trying to control her tears. She wanted to trust John completely and to be able to tell him that she did. But she couldn't. He was, after all, a Yankee stranger she'd known for such a short time. "Yes, I'm afraid I do. Even after last night, you're hardly more than a stranger."

Her words landed a severe blow to John's confidence in their budding relationship. "Is that all I am, Laurel, a stranger?"

She refused to look at him even though he still stroked her wrist, his hard chest almost touching her shoulder where he had kneeled beside her chair. "I can't finish Pappy Drew's biography now, and people will wonder why." She jerked her wrist out of John's grasp and clutched both hands in front of her. "The dream that I've carried in my heart for so long... I've wanted to see Johnny and Clarice's story written and published for as long as I can remember."

"You can still write their story. Dammit, honey, can't you see that all the truth will do is make it more romantic. Ol' J.T. gave up everything for the woman he loved."

Laurel jumped to her feet and glared at John. "I should have known you'd never understand. After all, what do you know about chivalry and honor and family pride?"

"So we're back to that? Honey, you don't know what you want. Your mind tells you that you want an old-fashioned Southern gentleman, and your heart tells you that you want some fantasy lover. But I'll just bet your body tells you that you want a rough, Yankee ex-sailor."

"Why don't you leave?" Laurel's voice trembled with anger and frustration. "Don't you think you've done enough damage?"

"Hellfire, are you crazy?" John bellowed as he took a step closer to Laurel and watched her back away from him. "We're talking about people who lived and died before our parents were born. What possible difference could it make to anyone that Johnny Drew committed bigamy?"

"I knew you didn't understand!"

"Dammit, Laurel, you can still write that biography. Tell the truth. People will be impressed that a man and woman would live with such a secret their whole lives because they loved each other. My God, woman, can't you understand that kind of passion?"

Laurel tensed but stayed securely at a distance from John. Even if he were touching her heart, he wasn't touching her physically, she thought. His words made sense to her, and that was frightening. She wanted to scream that yes, she understood that kind of passion. Only the turmoil of uncertainty raging within her was keeping her from throwing herself into John's arms and telling him that nothing mattered but the love she felt for him.

"It matters," Laurel cried, turning her back on John. "It matters to me."

"Be reasonable, honey," John said, desperately wanting to pick her up, throw her over his shoulder, and take her away from this house and this town, and this absurd notion of ancestor worship. "What you've found out today doesn't really change anything. It doesn't change the past for Clarice and Johnny. It doesn't change who you are. You're still a beautiful Southern belle whose great-great-grandmother fell in love with a Yankee and founded the Drew family.''

"A bastard family," Laurel said, her words tight and clipped.

"You don't believe that," John said. "In your heart, you know that the love Johnny and Clarice shared gave a legitimacy to their union that no legality ever could. Love unites and commits two people. In their hearts, Johnny and Clarice were man and wife."

"Their whole life together was a lie." Laurel kept her back to John, hoping he would leave her alone. She didn't want him to say the things that her own mind and heart were telling her, that she was beginning to believe. "Don't ask me to condone what they did." Slowly Laurel turned to face John. "They chose to live in sin for a lifetime, and now we, their descendants, have to deal with their shame."

"I give up," John said. "This whole thing is nothing but a bunch of bull. I happen to love you, but I have no intention of trying to fight through that wall of prejudice you've built around you. Stay right here in the old plantation house and wait around for some other fantasy lover. But, by God, what you need, Miss Laurel, is a flesh and blood man."

John scowled at Laurel, then turned and walked out of the parlor. Laurel was torn between wanting to run after John and wanting to throw herself onto the floor, ranting and raving like a madwoman. Too much had happened. More than she could deal with in a sane, rational manner. But one thought rang loud and clear through the pandemonium bombarding her mind—John had told her that he loved her.

Laurel ran into the hallway and toward the open front door. Her breathing quickened and her heartbeat accelerated as she rushed out onto the veranda. She opened her mouth to cry out to John just as he revved the motor of his Jag and shifted it into gear.

"John," Laurel cried, but her voice was a mere whisper, lost in the roar of the sports car's departure.

Laurel sagged against one of the huge white columns that graced the veranda. Perhaps it was for the best that John hadn't seen or heard her, she thought. If he'd stopped, if she'd had the chance to talk to him, what would she have said?

"I love you," she said quietly, knowing that only the sun and the soft summer breeze heard her declaration. Nothing that had happened today had changed that one fact—she loved John Mason.

Laurel turned and went inside the mansion. She looked down at the wide-plank cherry floor beneath her feet, a patina of age from numerous waxings giving it a lustrous surface. She walked past the solid maple doors leading into the gentlemen's parlor. The entrance hall suddenly seemed enormous and cold, almost alien.

She stood beside the trestle table centered between the two parlor entrances. Hesitant about entering the front parlor, she looked down at the table and immediately saw a small antique picture frame lying there. When she started to pick it up, splinters of broken glass fell from her hand onto the floor. She held the tintype in her palm and gazed down at the image of a young couple. She knew it was J. T. Andrews and his Ohio bride. John must have brought the picture with him today, Laurel thought. But why was it broken? And why had he left it?

She looked again at the bridal couple in the picture, and her heart ached for the somber pair who had posed before the camera. It had been a marriage of convenience, not love, and perhaps that had been the greatest sin of all.

Laurel took a deep breath, clasped the broken frame in her hand, and parted the double doors of the front parlor.

She moved slowly across the room, idly observing the small group of paintings that comprised her aunt's art collection.

Laurel's hand trembled as she neared the lord-and-lady English desk. On one end of the curved, raised top sat a small brass lamp, and on the other end rested a brass bud vase holding a single pink rose. She walked around to the front of the desk and looked down. It was lying there, just where she'd known it would be. Exactly where her Aunt Polly had placed it, as if she'd known Laurel would seek it out. Her hand hovered over the leather-bound journal before she reached out and touched it.

Clarice DuBois's diary. What if John Mason had never come to Tuscumbia on a quest for his elderly grandmother? That question invaded Laurel's mind, destroying her ability to think of anything else. And what if, Laurel wondered, J. T. Andrews had never been wounded during the Civil War and nursed back to health by a young Southern girl?

Laurel sat down in the red leather wing chair at the desk, lay the tintype in her lap, picked up the diary, and clutched it to her bosom.

"Help me, Grandmother Clarice. Help me to be as strong as you were."

The journal felt warm and alive as it lay against her heart, and, somehow she knew that reading it from beginning to end was the only way she could come to terms with the past as well as the present. Clarice DuBois had claimed her Yankee lover. Laurel wondered if she had ever regretted that choice.

Nine

———

Laurel looked at the cloudy afternoon sky as she walked with Aunt Polly to the '77 Buick Riviera parked at the back of the house. Laurel knew her aunt would drive the big, gas-guzzling car for the rest of her life because Uncle William had bought the car new a few years before his death.

Polly opened the back door and placed a small overnight bag on the floor, then turned to face Laurel. "I should be home before noon tomorrow. I advise you to take full advantage of my absence."

"Aunt Polly, I wish you wouldn't go." Laurel nodded toward the black clouds forming in the eastern sky. "You and Clintelle will get drenched if you go out tonight. The weather forecast said that we're in for quite a summer storm."

"Pooh. You young folks think a little wet weather should keep us old folks from having a night on the town. Clintelle and Peter have already made arrangements with Harvey."

"Harvey Grimes drinks. Y'all could have a wreck on the way to or from the movies. I don't think this is a good idea."

"Laurel, I'm going to Sheffield to spend the night with Clintelle." Polly took her niece's hand and patted it gently. "We have a double date for dinner and the movies. This is something I do almost every month, and you've never had any objections before. Besides, Peter always drives."

"It's going to rain."

"Rain is very romantic. You and I both know that the only reason you don't want me to go is because you're afraid to call John. I'm giving you the opportunity to be alone with him, to have him stay the night, and you're afraid."

"I have no intention of letting him spend the night here."

Polly opened the car door and threw her purse onto the front seat. "Call John. Tell him you want to talk. If you can pour out your heart and soul to Carter Moody, you can darn well tell John that you love him."

"I called Carter and asked him to come over last night because I needed someone to talk to about this mess."

"You talked to me," Aunt Polly said. "I gave you better advice than Carter did."

"When I told Carter the entire story, he simply suggested that I would be wise not to let the whole world know the truth about Pappy Drew. He did point out that it would be a great shock to Mamma and Daddy."

"Hmmph. Forget everything Carter said, and call John."

"What if he's already left town?"

"He hasn't. I called his motel this morning."

"You didn't!"

Polly got inside the Riviera and slammed the door. She smiled at her niece and waved goodbye as she started the engine.

Laurel stepped away from the car and waved, feeling totally alone and uncertain. She stood on the brick driveway until her aunt drove off, then she walked over and sat down in the huge fan-backed wicker chair on the rear veranda.

With her heart and mind in turmoil, she lay her head back and closed her eyes, her body absorbing the humid heat of the cloudy July afternoon. She didn't want to make any decisions today. It was too soon. She needed more time, but time was the one thing she didn't have. She was surprised that John was still in town. She'd expected him to leave for Florida after he'd stormed out of the house. Was he waiting for her to call? Did he expect her to make the first move?

After he'd left yesterday, and she'd found where Aunt Polly put Clarice DuBois's diary, she sat in the front parlor for hours reading and rereading every word. She became intimately acquainted with her great-great-grandmother in those hours of early evening. As twilight surrounded the plantation house, Laurel had gone into the kitchen and found Aunt Polly preparing supper. They'd talked for hours, Laurel pouring out all her anger and fear, all her hurt and disappointment.

Then she had called Carter. They had been friends all their lives, and she knew he understood her outlook on life better than anyone. They were a great deal alike, she and Carter, and she valued his opinion. He'd listened patiently while she told him the whole story—how Aunt Polly had known the truth for years and had hidden the diary; how Laurel was torn between completing her book and never finishing it; and that she loved John Mason but was afraid to trust her future to him.

Laurel had spent a restless, sleepless night, remembering the scene with John after she'd read to him out of the diary, reliving the passion of their lovemaking, and visualizing a Johnny Drew painted so vividly by Clarice's loving words.

There was no denying that J. T. Andrews had been a bigamist, and that Clarice had lived her whole life protecting those she loved from a secret that could have destroyed them. Why, Laurel wondered, had Clarice felt the need to expose the truth in her old age? Had any one of her three sons ever read the diary? Had Clarice hidden the journal in the secret compartment of her trunk, or had one of her sons? The questions filled Laurel's mind, but one question gripped her heart. What would John Mason do with the information he'd learned?

John picked up the enormous bouquet of white roses from the passenger seat of his Jag. It had been a long time since he'd bought flowers for a woman, so long ago he couldn't even remember. But Laurel Drew was the kind of woman who would not only appreciate flowers of apology, she'd expect them.

With flowers in hand and the tattered nerves of a rejected suitor, John stepped up on the front veranda and rang the door chimes. He waited for endless moments, and when no one answered, he rang again. Where the hell was she? he wondered. When Aunt Polly called, she'd assured him that Laurel would be here, and that she'd be alone.

He knew his less then gentlemanly departure yesterday had probably ruined any chance he'd ever had with Laurel. He'd tossed and turned in his motel bed half the night, then had finally given up on getting any sleep and had gone to an all-night coffee shop and filled his system with caffeine and nicotine.

The one clear thought he couldn't deny was that he loved Laurel. He wouldn't leave Tuscumbia until he'd made her understand that the past didn't matter. Not his past or hers. Not Johnny Drew's and J. T. Andrews's. All his life, he'd settled for less than what he really wanted. He had let other people's actions dominate his life. He'd allowed his grandfather's overbearing ways to run him away from home. He'd let Cassie's rejection turn his heart to stone and make him afraid to risk loving another woman. He'd let his devotion to his grandmother give him second thoughts about what he wanted to do with the rest of his life. He'd be damned if he'd let Laurel's obsession with her non-too-illustrious ancestor ruin their chance for a lifetime together.

John finally decided that Laurel was probably in the yard somewhere, perhaps in the gardens. He rounded the corner of the house and caught a glimpse of the back veranda. Laurel sat in the regal wicker chair. The sunlight glistened on her upturned face, illuminating the teardrops falling from her eyes. Oh, God, she's crying, he thought as he stood perfectly still watching her from a safe distance, and at an angle that kept his presence unnoticeable.

She was, without a doubt, the most beautiful, desirable woman he'd ever known. Sitting there in full sunlight without any makeup, her creamy complexion, her black brows and lashes, her naturally pink lips needed no artificial help. Just looking at her filled his heart with wonder and aroused his body with loving desire. Her breasts generously filled the hand-smocked top of her strapless pink sundress, and the fitted waist nipped her middle to minuscule proportions. Her tanned legs were bare, the bottom of her skirt hiked up slightly above one knee, revealing several inches of her luscious thighs.

He couldn't stop looking at her, feasting on her beauty. Suddenly he felt afraid. What would he do if she refused to listen to him, if she listened and then rejected him? The thought of losing her was more than he could bear.

Laurel brought her hands to her face and wiped away the tears with open palms. She ran her fingers into her hair above her ears and bowed her head. "Oh, John... John... Johnny," she whispered his name and buried her face in her hands.

The sound of her voice calling his name tore into her very soul. She was in pain, and he knew he was the source of her agony. He forced himself to move, to take the few steps that put him in full view. When she didn't look up, he cleared his throat. His fist tightened on the bouquet in his hand. "Laurel."

She jerked her head up and stared at him with wide eyes.

He walked up the steps, stopping just as his feet touched the veranda. "I needed to see you."

Laurel clutched her hands in front of her, then dropped them to her lap. "You should have called," she said, realizing how ridiculous the statement was the minute she'd uttered it.

He held the bouquet out and moved over to stand directly in front of her chair. "Aunt Polly said white roses are your favorite."

She stared at the flowers as if they were objects she'd never seen. "They're beautiful."

"You're beautiful."

She reached out, accepting the roses while John stood gazing down at her. "Thank you." She took the flowers and lay them on the small wicker table at her side.

"Can I stay?" he asked, silently praying that she'd look at him.

With her eyes focused on her lap, Laurel sighed. "I...I'm not sure it would do any good. There is so much standing between us."

John dropped to his knees before her. He took her hands into his as they rested against her thighs. "I love you, Laurel, and I think you love me. Don't we owe it to ourselves to try?"

Look at me, dammit, his heart cried out as he felt her hands trembling within his grasp.

Laurel raised her head slightly, lifting her eyes to meet his. "We can start by talking, by being honest."

"Agreed."

"I can't think straight when you're touching me," she admitted.

He released her hands and stood up. "Better?"

"Yes, thank you." She motioned toward the other fan-backed wicker chair a few feet away. "Please, sit down."

"Always the proper Southern lady." He sat down, his dark eyes never leaving her face for a moment.

"Yes, it's difficult for me to forget the manners instilled in me as a child."

"Your old-fashioned manners are delightful, Laurel. I'd never want to see them change."

"Before...before I discuss the J.T./Johnny issue, I have to know something."

"Anything," he said, knowing that he was prepared to bare his soul to this woman if that's what it took to win her love and trust.

"You say that you love me. Just exactly what does that mean? Are you offering me a brief affair or—"

"Dammit all, woman, how can you ask me such a thing?" John jumped to his feet, his black eyes fierce. "I love you. L-O-V-E. As in forever after. From the moment I saw you dripping wet in that purple bathing suit, no other woman has existed for me."

"John?"

"I want to spend the rest of my life with you." He lifted her out of the chair, his big hands gripping her waist.

Hesitantly, she placed her hands on his shoulders and smiled up at him. "Oh."

"I think it's my turn now," he said, pulling her a fraction closer.

"What?"

"I need to know that I don't have any competition."

"I love Carter like a brother. That's all there's ever been between us."

"I'm not talking about Moody. I'm talking about your fantasy lover."

When Laurel didn't reply, John felt as if his heart had stopped beating.

"I want you to understand about that," she said. "I have to tell you the truth since we're being honest with each other."

"I'm not sure I want to know, now."

"I need for you to know." When he tried to pull her closer, she resisted. "Let's take a walk. I won't be able to tell you anything if you keep holding me like this."

Side by side, but not physically touching, Laurel and John walked across the backyard and through the flower garden. Rows of Aunt Polly's prize rosebushes filled the muggy summer air with their sweet fragrance.

"Come on," Laurel said as she led John past the gardens and toward the woods. "There's a path through Drew Woods. Tale has it that the original path was made by Chickasaw Indians who lived on this land two hundred years ago."

Laurel wasn't sure why she felt it would be easier to tell John about her obsession with Johnny Drew and her own fantasized Yankee lover once they were cocooned within the woods. All her life she'd felt an affinity with nature, a security and peace in the solitude she found in the shady grove deep within these woods. As a child she had sat on a huge rock beside a small, underground spring and wrote silly, romantic poetry about Johnny and Clarice and about a mysterious Yankee lover. Perhaps that was why she wanted this private talk with John Mason, why she felt the need to share her most secret dreams with him beneath the sheltering arms of ancient trees.

She detected the faint sound of running water moments before their feet encountered the soggy earth where the spring issued forth its mineral water. She moved quickly toward the smooth boulder where she'd spent endless hours sitting and absorbing nature.

"Watch out for the mud," Laurel said, pointing to the ground. "There's a spring here by the rocks. Even in July the ground stays wet."

A clap of distant thunder disturbed the tranquility, and dark storm clouds swirled threateningly in the sky. A hot, clammy breeze stirred through the trees. Laurel wiped the sweat from her cheeks as she sat down on the rock.

"Sit beside me. There's room." She patted the smooth surface of the moss-covered stone.

He eased himself down beside her. "Tell me about your fantasy lover and about me."

Laurel didn't look at him but out into the woods. She rested her hands on her knees and crossed her legs at the ankles. "As long as I can remember, I've dreamed of having a dashing, Yankee lover like Clarice had. When I was a little girl, it was an innocent child's dream. Like a fairy tale. I'd been weaned on the Johnny Drew legend."

"And when you grew up and became a woman?"

"Every boy I ever dated fell short of my fantasized hero. I think one of the reasons I allowed myself to get involved with Scott was because he was so different. I thought he . . . well, that he was the man of my dreams."

"But he wasn't."

"He was my nightmare."

"And what am I, Laurel?"

"You, John Mason, are my Yankee lover, the man I've dreamed of all my life, but...but sometimes when I look at you, I see Johnny Drew. Your smile is his smile. I love and want you, but—"

"We can work through this, honey. You can prove to both of us that I'm the man you love."

"I want to, but I'm afraid. There's so much standing between us. So many lies, so many—"

"Dammit, Laurel, there is nothing wrong between us that we can't work out." John grasped her chin in his hand. "I love you and I want you, but you're going to have to meet me halfway."

She pulled away and stood up. The humid breeze grew stronger, the trees and brush bending to its force. "We're too different. We come from such opposite backgrounds.

Our life-styles are not compatible. One of us would have to completely change."

John stood up. Loud thunder and sizzling lightning issued summer storm warnings. "We could compromise. We could each change a little."

"You'd hate living here in Tuscumbia. You'd never make the kind of sacrifices Johnny Drew did."

Angry, John glared at the stubborn woman he loved. "You mean J. T. Andrews, don't you?"

"Yes, I mean John Terrence Andrews!" Laurel screamed. "There, I've said it. I've admitted that Johnny Drew was a romantic dream, a fantasy man who never existed. Are you satisfied?"

"You satisfy me, Laurel, like no other woman ever has. Even when you call me Johnny, I know that I'm the man who's giving you pleasure, the man you want. I can be the only man in your heart, if you'll just give me the chance."

Her soft, violet eyes turned deep purple as they hardened into a searching stare. Everything around them vanished into a blur as the world shrank to encompass only John Mason's rugged face and the fierce hunger she saw in his black eyes. Dammit, he excited her. He more than excited her. The sight and scent of him there beside her lit flames of longing deep within her. The feminine needs crying out for John's touch both tempted and frightened Laurel.

"Can you deny that you want me?" His eyes issued a dare. He didn't move, didn't touch her, but he could feel her body reacting to his nearness.

She felt pinpricks of rain hit her face but was so absorbed in the sexual battle going on between John and herself that she didn't immediately react to their signal. "Please, don't do this to me."

"I haven't done anything to you . . . yet."

"Let me go."

"I'm not even touching you, honey." John felt rain-drops moistening his skin as thunder and lighting ravaged the darkening summer sky.

Laurel told herself to move, to walk away and never look back. But her body refused to obey the command of her mind when her heart was screaming for her to surrender. "I'm going to the house. It's raining," she said as if that fact had something to do with what was happening between them.

"I'm so hungry for you, Laurel. I want you so much."

"Why do you say things like that to me when I've asked you not to?"

"I want your mouth on mine. I want to taste you . . . feel you . . . love you."

Laurel cried out, the fury within her as wild and natural as the rainstorm's fervor. She swayed toward him as rain drenched her body, adhering her dress to her skin. Misty air whirled around them as their wet forms trembled with desire.

"Now," he groaned, reaching out and pulling her against him.

Her mouth opened the moment their bodies touched. He took her invitation, kissing her with a force that shook them both, his tongue hard and demanding. She grasped his shoulders trying to steady herself, then flung her arms around him, threading her fingers through his thick, blond hair. His big hands caressed the smoothness of her bare back. The kiss went on and on until another bolt of lightning struck nearby. John broke the kiss, resting his forehead against Laurel's.

"Kiss me again," she pleaded huskily.

He nipped at her lips with his teeth, and a sensual shiver ran through him. "Do you love me, Laurel?"

"Oh, God, yes. Yes, yes, yes."

"Then show me."

She stared at him, her eyes questioning his command. Then she stepped away from him, her fingers reaching out to touch his chest. Slowly, as the rain continued to pour down over them, Laurel unbuttoned John's shirt and pushed it apart. She tugged the bodice of her strapless sundress down to her waist, exposing her high, full breasts.

"Laurel...Laurel...."

"Help me. I..." she murmured, her skin sizzling from inner heat and outer moisture.

He pulled her against him, his hair-roughened chest uniting with her creamy flesh. "I've been dying to feel you against me like this."

With their half-naked bodies luxuriating in the union, John kissed her again. While his mouth feasted on hers, he swung her up into his arms and held her possessively. With her arms around his neck and her lips clinging to his, Laurel whispered his name as he walked through the woods and back toward the plantation house.

He stepped up onto the back veranda and lowered Laurel to her feet, her wet body gliding down his, her slick breasts cleaving to his chest. He clutched her hips, drawing her against his manhood. She trembled with fear and longing. He took her face in his hands and began a series of adoring kisses from her forehead to her chin.

"I want to make love with you," he said.

"Oh, John, I want that, too."

Laurel took his big hand in her small one and led him across the veranda and into the house. She knew, in her heart, that she had finally found the courage to claim her Yankee lover.

Ten

___

They stood in the back hallway, steamy darkness surrounding their wet bodies. A hazy radiance filtered into the area from the remaining daylight outside. John released Laurel's hand when they neared the back staircase. She turned to face him, her eyes pure velvet softness, her pink lips a seductive invitation.

He didn't touch her as his gaze focused first on her face and then moved slowly down to her exposed breasts. Dammit all, he wanted her here and now, in the hallway, on the floor, on the steps, backed up against a wall. His thoughts were savage, almost animalistic, and he fought to control them. He'd never known such raging hunger for a woman, but this hunger was combined with other emotions. He loved Laurel. He wanted to prove to her how much.

"Are you sure about this?" he asked, praying that she wouldn't change her mind.

"I've waited all my life for you, John Mason, and no matter what tomorrow brings, I want this. I want you." Her heart told her that John was unique, special, and the emotions he evoked within her made her feel special.

"Laurel...."

She touched his bare chest, her fingers gliding through his chest hair. "I love your chest. Your body is so hard, but your hair is so soft." Her voice was almost a purr.

"God, woman, do you know what it does to me when you touch me like that?"

Boldly, Laurel slid her hand down his chest and past his belt, stopping between his waist and his manhood. "My touch arouses you."

"For a woman with so little experience, you certainly are a wanton." He covered her fondling hand with his, moving it lower, pressing her palm downward to cover him.

Was she acting like a wanton? Laurel wondered. Somehow, with John, she felt wild and free, as if instincts alone were guiding her. She was woman. He was man. And everything they said and did was an expression of love, both sexual and spiritual.

He looked at her, his eyes cloudy with longing, as he closed the minute distance between them and crushed her against his damp chest. He brushed his lips against her warm, wet neck.

She threw her head backward, tingling with womanly perception as his mouth and tongue explored the tender skin of her neck and throat. "I feel like I'm on fire," she moaned as she struggled to unzip his jeans.

"Laurel...Laurel...." he groaned against her parted lips as his hands closed over her breasts.

"Yes, yes," she sighed, her arms reaching upward to circle his neck.

"Mine," he whispered hoarsely, planting quick, frenzied kisses on her lips, her cheeks, her eyes.

Laurel ran her hands across the firm width of his body from strong neck to broad shoulders, her fingers trembling in their compulsive caresses. His shudders revealed the power of her control over him. His fingers bit into the softness of her rounded bottom as he pushed his hands beneath her sundress and drew her to the hardening strength in his lower body.

"John . . . please. . . ." She wanted to be closer, needed to be a part of him.

Aggressively, she pressed her lips to his, offering her mouth. He accepted, gently pushing his tongue against her teeth, slowly moving into her sweet moistness. She groaned, as his tongue plunged harder and deeper, bringing a response from her own tongue.

John tugged at the wet material of her dress, awkwardly pulling it down and off her body. Laurel raised her feet slightly, helping him rid her of her clothing. He slipped his hand inside her damp panties and drew circles over her abdomen before sliding up to cup her breasts. He squeezed gently, kneaded tenderly. He took both rigid points between his thumbs and forefingers, pinching, releasing, pinching again. Her breasts ached, the pleasure so intense it was almost pain. He continued the attack on her nipples, drawing her body under his masculine control.

Laurel kissed his jaw, her tongue making passionate forays on his hair-stubbled flesh.

His hands left her breasts, gradually easing down to her waist. He slipped his hand inside her panties, fondling her, his hand pressing. "I want to look at you," he said, sliding his fingers inside her. "I don't want anything between us." With his free hand, he shrugged his wet shirt off his shoulders and threw it on the floor.

She swayed on her feet, her knees weakening when he moved his fingers in and out, massaging the nub of her desire. "You're so soft, so incredibly soft. . . ." he said.

Laurel eased her hand inside his jeans and snuggled her fingers around his covered manhood. "I want to see you, too," she said, her voice an impassioned whimper.

"God, Laurel! I've got to have you." He was lost to his own overwhelming needs as he ripped her silky panties away from her body and lifted her into his arms, burying his face against her breasts.

She clung to him, her head resting on his shoulder, her body throbbing with an ache she knew only he could appease. She tried to think, but her mind refused to function. Her aroused body was in charge and would not allow sensible thoughts to prevent the satisfaction it craved.

"Love me, John . . . love me."

"Oh, yes, sweet baby, I have every intention of loving you." His voice was a deep, thick sound, which stimulated her to fever pitch. "I'll take it slow and easy."

"No," she said, dying for the touch of his lips on her body. "That's not how I want it. I ache . . . oh, John, I ache."

"Not here, in the hall, on the floor." He made one last effort at being a sane, reasonable man, all the while knowing he couldn't stand much more.

"Yes. Here. Now." Her breath was a ragged whisper against his skin. "We've got all night to make slow, easy love in a bed upstairs."

"I don't want to hurt you." As he spoke, he bent to his knees and lowered her to the wooden floor.

"I want you so," she told him as he hovered above her, feasting on the sight of her ripe, utterly female body.

He squeezed her breasts and trembled when her body jerked convulsively. "That's it, Laurel, want me."

"I do. If you stop, I think I'll die."

"Don't worry," he assured her as he pulled his jeans down his legs and tossed them aside. "Nothing on earth could stop me now."

John's hands moved from breasts to hips to thighs in a gentle exploration. Laurel was unaware of the enticing little moans escaping from her throat when his tongue touched the tip of one throbbing breast, her body arching upward, straining for that fundamental joining. His own body acknowledged the primitive hunger raging like an uncontrollable wildfire through his veins. He knew he had to take her, and soon, or he would burst into a thousand tortured pieces.

He moved quickly, lifting up just enough to accommodate the easier removal of his briefs. Laurel whimpered a frustrated cry of protest, her hands blindly clinging, her hips undulating rhythmically.

"Hush, sweet baby. I've got to get rid of these," he said, his breath ragged with desire. "I'm not leaving you."

His briefs joined her panties as he lowered himself onto her, one leg separating her thighs, his starving mouth feasting on her parted lips.

John forced himself to slow down, to try to think, but his body urged him on, and his words to Laurel pleaded for her to respond. "That's it, baby, open up. Give yourself to me."

With a provocative movement of complete surrender, Laurel relaxed, submitting herself to his possession while she claimed him for her own. With one swift thrust, he entered her, tearing from her lips a cry of savage pleasure.

He felt her body grip him as he lost himself inside her. "Laurel . . . Laurel . . . ."

"John . . . Johnny . . . ." She said his name in a murmured sigh, her eyes, so filled with love, looking up at him.

"There's never going to be anyone else for either of us," he said, then his lips moved over hers, demanding and receiving their total cooperation, just as his masculinity began its deep, powerful drive into her moist softness.

It was everything and more. Laurel reveled in the knowledge that John was both a passionate and considerate lover, giving as much as he took, bringing her closer and closer to ultimate fulfillment.

"Easy, baby, easy," he said, his hands lifting her hips higher as his maleness made the final earth-shattering lunges, bringing her to completion.

Laurel's body shook with spasms of release while John continued the stroking moves that brought wave after wave

of ecstasy washing over her. And just as she went limp,
sharp sensations dulling to satiation, John groaned and
drove into her one final time, shuddering with the force of
his satisfaction. His manly grunts mingled with her feminine sighs in the stillness of the humid summer air.

He held her close against him as he rolled to his side, his
mouth lost in the clean sweetness of her still damp hair. She
could feel the steady beat of his heart where her hand rested
on his chest.

"We're very, very good together, aren't we?" she asked,
already knowing the answer.

"Oh, honey, that's the understatement of the century. We
are . . . fantastic together."

"There's a bed upstairs," she said, laughing.

"I'm not sure I've got the energy to walk up the stairs."

"It was Clarice and Johnny's bed," she told him,
searching his face for a reaction.

"Mmm . . . mmm. Are you trying to tell me something?"
He moved his fingers down the side of her hip, idly caressing her bare skin.

"If I make love to you in that bed, I'll be giving you not
just my body, or even my heart, but my soul."

"Laurel?" His hand stilled on her warm flesh. He raised
himself on one elbow and looked down at her.

"You're my destiny, John Mason, and I'm yours. Just as
our ancestors sealed their fate in that old tester bed, so will
we."

"Who and what am I to you, Laurel?"

"You, Johnny, are my Yankee lover, my fantasy, the man
I've waited for all my life."

"I'm a Yankee, that's true, and I'm most definitely your
lover, but I'm not a fantasy, honey. I'm a flesh and blood
man, an ordinary human being."

Laurel put her arms around his neck and drew his head
down to hers. She brushed her lips across his. "I know ex-

actly how human you are, but believe me, you're not ordinary."

"What on earth am I going to do with you, my romantic little Southern belle?"

"You're going to take me upstairs and spend the night teaching me how to be the perfect lover for you."

John couldn't believe he was ready for her again. The nearness of her naked body, the touch of her flesh against his, the invitation of her words, awakened anew the desire he'd only moments before sated.

"Let's go upstairs, and I'll give you lesson number two," John said.

The first thing Laurel realized was that it had stopped raining, and the second thing she realized was that she was naked. She smiled to herself, remembering the hours that had gone before, the aching sweet moments of passion she'd shared with John. She stretched lazily beneath the sheet before pushing herself into a sitting position. I'm so happy, she thought, happier than I've ever been in my entire life. She was in love, wildly, passionately in love with the most wonderful man in the world. John had brought her to life, had given her a confidence in her sexuality that no one could ever take away from her.

She wished she could turn on a light and look at him as he lay sleeping beside her in the kingly antique bed. She ran one hand up the line-fold panels of the carved headboard. Grandmother Clarice had conceived and given birth to three sons in this bed, Laurel thought. Someday she hoped to conceive John's child in this very bed.

The thought of marrying John and giving him a child sent conflicting images through Laurel's mind. Now that she loved John, there could never be another man for her, and yet she wondered if he was the kind of man who could fit into her life here in Tuscumbia and stay committed to her forever. She wished that she could escape from the knowledge that her family and friends would consider John beneath them socially. It shouldn't matter, she told herself. I love him, and I'm not going to lose him.

She reached out, running her other hand up and down the polished surface of one rope-turned bedpost. She didn't want to give up the life she'd always known. Her heritage was an important part of who and what she was. She'd just have to persuade John to become a part of that life.

Laurel felt him stir beside her, his big body turning over, his bare chest tempting her fingers. Hesitantly, she gave in to temptation and touched him. He groaned, but his eyes remained closed.

"Laurel?" he asked so quietly that at first she thought he was talking in his sleep but knew he was awake when she felt his lips move up the side of her body. His tongue left a wet trail from her waist to the outer swell of her breast. "What are you doing sitting up? You're not supposed to be out of my arms."

She lay down and snuggled close to him. He pulled her closer, her firm breasts pressing against his chest. "I don't ever want to be out of your arms," she said.

"I love you, Laurel. More than anything." His voice was like a sensuous caress to her heart, a precious commitment to her soul.

"I never dreamed that making love could be like this," she said, her face slightly flushed.

"Neither did I. I guess when two people love each other the way we do, the loving can be perfect." He moved his hands up her stomach, gliding over silky skin until they stopped beneath the fullness of her bosom.

She wanted him to take her breasts in his hands, to rub his calloused thumbs across her aching nipples, to love her there with his mouth.

As if he'd read her mind, he cupped the soft weight of her. His fingers teased the nubs to rigid points as his tongue drew moist patterns across her collarbone, then moved ever so gradually downward.

They had already made love twice, but it wasn't enough, she thought. It would never be enough for either of them. It was as if they'd known each other forever, each holding their love a secret within their hearts. Their joining had been a culmination building since the dawn of time.

"I want you." John's words were almost lost against her open mouth as his lips pressed possessively against hers. He raised himself over her, nudging her thighs apart with his knee. The gentleness with which he'd taken her the second time was gone, replaced by the passionate intensity of their first loving.

She moaned as the heaviness of his body came down on her, his tongue lunging repeatedly into the waiting dampness of her eager mouth.

He ended the kiss as he whispered against her neck, "I want to lose myself inside you."

He looked down, seeing her long hair shining like polished ebony around her shoulders, her beautiful face glowing with anticipation, and her eyes alight with the depth of her love for him. "I want to fill you, to make you a part of me. Oh, honey, I want to take you quickly this time."

Arching her feverishly aroused body up toward the hairroughened ruggedness of his, she answered his plea, "Yes, yes. Take me now!"

As if pushed beyond the limit of his control by her demand, he drove into her with a barbaric wildness that commanded her body to respond with equal fervor, both of them moaning their pleasure, crying out their passion. He thought he would go crazy enjoying the feel of her sheathing him, encompassing him. She was so hot, so wet, so totally giving that he surged harder and faster, faster and harder.

"Good ... so good...." he moaned.

"Oh, Johnny...."

The tempo of their lovemaking increased to a fury of pleasure so intense that John clasped her hips in his hands, forging them into one entity. Desire beyond reason, joy beyond bearing, their loving continued until John was so lost in the spasms of his own release, he was only vaguely aware of the trembling force of Laurel's, until she called his name, her fingers grasping his firm buttocks.

He rested his spent body atop hers as she held him close. He eased off her, resting at her side, kissing her again and again while he listened to her whispered words of love. For a long time they lay quietly, their fingers gently caressing each other, their closed eyelids opening occasionally so each could enjoy the look of complete fulfillment on the other's face.

Laurel rested in his arms, floating somewhere in that blissful satiation between earth and paradise. Tomorrow, she thought, tomorrow we'll work out all our problems. Tomorrow we'll make plans for the future. She snuggled closer, blissfully happy in the arms of the man she loved.

Eleven

Laurel loosened the towel from around her head and briskly rubbed her wet hair as she walked into the kitchen. She hung the damp towel on the back of a cane-bottomed chair and tightened the belt of her shorty cotton robe. When she'd checked her digital alarm before taking a shower, she'd realized the power had gone off and come back on sometime during the night. But she knew it was already after ten because the antique grandfather clock in the downstairs hallway had chimed a few minutes ago when she'd stood over her sleeping lover, wondering whether or not she should awaken him. She'd decided to let him sleep while she prepared breakfast for the two of them. This would be their first morning-after together, and she wanted it to be very special.

She set the coffeemaker, then before retrieving the staples she needed from the refrigerator, she decided to call Aunt Polly and ask her not to come home just yet. She supposed she would have to tell her aunt the truth, but it would be worth it to have a few more hours alone with John. Laurel picked up the receiver and began dialing Clintelle Simpson's number. Suddenly she realized the phone was dead. The storm probably knocked out the telephone lines, she thought. Oh, well, maybe I'd better make breakfast for three.

While ham and eggs sizzled on the stove and biscuits browned in the oven, Laurel walked outside onto the back veranda. The whole world was bright and fresh, cleansed by the night's rain. But July sunshine had already absorbed most of the excess moisture and created a steaminess Laurel could almost see. Her wandering eyes caught sight of the bouquet of white roses John had given her yesterday. She was sorry she'd forgotten about them and left them to withstand the storm. Some of the roses were scattered in pieces across the veranda, but several undisturbed buds remained on the table. She picked them up and held them to her nose, breathing in their uniquely sweet scent.

Just as she opened the back door, she heard the sound of a car. She turned around and saw her aunt's blue Riviera as it pulled into the back driveway.

Damn, Laurel thought, there's nothing to do now but tell her everything and see if she won't discreetly disappear for a few hours.

Laurel rushed down the steps, hoping to catch her aunt before she got out of the car, hoping she could give her a short explanation with a promise for more details later. Just as Polly Drew opened the car door, Laurel reached the end of the walkway.

"Good Lord, girl, it's nearly noon and you're still in your housecoat," the old woman said, a Cheshire cat smile on her face as she put one foot on the ground. "Your being undressed wouldn't have anything to do with John Mason's car being parked out front, would it?"

"Yes, it would," Laurel admitted, trying not to grin like an idiot. "Would you please go somewhere else for a few hours? You could drive over to the Yancey's and have a nice long visit with Wheeler.''

Polly put her other foot on the ground and stepped out of the car, a newspaper clasped in one hand. "I know you want to be alone with John, but I'm afraid I'm going to have to stay.''

"Aunt Polly," Laurel groaned, planting her hands on her hips. "What you've been wanting to happen has finally happened, but John and I have a few loose ends to tie up.''

Polly slammed the car door and turned to face Laurel. "I understand all that, but I'm afraid we have a much more pressing matter to take care of first.''

"What on earth are you talking about?''

"This." Polly opened the newspaper and handed it to Laurel. "I've been trying to call you for hours. You're lucky the phone's out of order because once it's fixed we're in for it.''

Laurel took the *Colbert Daily News* and scanned the headlines. Nothing of real interest there, she thought. Her eyes moved up and down and across. Then she saw it. "Oh, my God!" she cried, letting the cherished rosebuds she held fall to the ground.

"The whole town is buzzing with the news. Harvey called me at the crack of dawn. It seems he'd already received several phone calls. I shudder in horror to think of your mamma and daddy's reaction when they get home. Lord, help us all.''

Polly put her arm around Laurel and led her toward the veranda. When she neared the steps, Laurel sat down in a slump, grasping the open newspaper.

"Legendary Johnny Drew Bigamist," Laurel read, cringing as she continued slowly. "A secret diary hidden in Clarice DuBois Drew's trunk was recently discovered by a member of the family.''

"It's all there," Polly said, looking down at her niece and shaking her head sympathetically. "Every sordid little detail, but nothing about the reasons why he did it or why he and Clarice felt justified.''

Laurel bit her bottom lip, trying unsuccessfully not to cry. ''J. T. Andrews not only deserted the Union army, but his pregnant young wife.'' Laurel choked on the words. ''How could this have happened? Who could have told Mabel Suggs about this?''

''I think the list of suspects are pretty well narrowed down to four, don't you think?''

''Aunt Polly, you . . . you didn't . . .''

''Laurel Drew!'' the old woman snapped. ''I'm ashamed that you'd think such a thing.''

''I'm sorry, but you do have a tendency to . . . to talk about things you shouldn't.''

''That may well be true, but I could never have done something like this . . . something that would have hurt you.'' Polly sniffed the air, as if detecting some unpleasant odor. ''Laurel, are you cooking something? I think I smell smoke.''

''Oh, Lord!'' Laurel jumped to her feet and ran inside to the kitchen. The entire room was filled with smoke, dark puffs swirling around the stove. Flames shot up from the electric-eye around a skillet filled with sliced ham.

Panic raced through Laurel's befuddled brain. The fire extinguisher, she thought. Get the fire extinguisher. She dropped the newspaper and ran to the pantry, grabbed the extinguisher, and came back into the room. Just as she neared the stove, Aunt Polly walked in the back door and John came into the kitchen through the dining room. The moment John saw what was happening, he grabbed the fire extinguisher from Laurel, issued a warning for her to get out of the way, and promptly put out the fire.

Polly moved across the room and opened both windows. Laurel stood beside the kitchen table, her eyes glued to John as if she were in a trance. He set the extinguisher down on the table and pulled Laurel into his arms.

"Honey, are you all right?"

Laurel stood there in his arms, her body rigid, her violet eyes staring up at him.

"She came outside to meet me and forgot she had breakfast cooking in here," Polly said. "Let me get you a glass of water, Laurel. You look a bit pale."

"It's all right now," John said. "The fire's out. No real damage done." He couldn't understand why she was so tense, so silent. It was as if far more were wrong than the crisis that had just ended. "Laurel, for Pete's sake, snap out of it."

"Do you want to tell him, or should I?" Polly asked.

Laurel pulled out of John's arms and knelt to retrieve the newspaper she'd dropped on the floor. She looked at him accusingly as she held the paper out to him.

His gaze moved from Laurel to the paper to Aunt Polly and back to Laurel. "What is it?"

"Read." Laurel cleared her throat. "Read the paper. Front page."

John quickly saw the article and skimmed just enough to get the gist of it. "Dammit!"

Laurel pulled a chair out from the table and sat down. She felt numb. Cold. She wondered how she could feel so cold when hot outdoor air drifted through the open window to mix with the heat left from the accidental fire.

One thought kept racing through Laurel's mind—four people had known the whole truth about Johnny Drew and J. T. Andrews. She didn't want to believe the obvious, but the evidence was stacked against him.

"Why?" Laurel asked, her voice a cracked whisper.

"What?" John's voice blended with Polly's when they both asked the question.

"Why did you think it necessary to tell the *Daily* . . . I thought . . . I'd hoped you wouldn't . . . only your grandmother . . . why?" Laurel's words were a jumbled mass of questions and sobs.

"Laurel!" Polly Drew gasped.

John dropped to his knees in front of Laurel. "You can't mean to say that you think I told this reporter, this Mabel Suggs, about the diary, about J. T. Andrews?"

Laurel jerked away from him when John tried to take her hands.

The telephone's distinct ring momentarily immobilized all three people. When the phone continued ringing, Polly walked across the room and picked up the receiver.

"Yes. No, I'm sorry. No. The family has no comment to make at this time." Polly placed the phone back on the wall rack.

"Who?" Laurel asked, her body tightening as she clutched her hands together and held them to her breast.

"The local TV news." Polly's somber expression showed her concern. "We may have to unplug that thing now that it's back in working order."

John took Laurel's wrists in his hands. "Look at me, dammit. I did not give that story to the newspaper. I haven't told anyone about the diary or about what I suspected. Do you hear me?"

Laurel nodded her head affirmatively, but her eyes were cold and unseeing as she stared at John. "Then who?" she asked. "Only four of us knew. Aunt Polly didn't. I didn't."

"Four?" John asked. "Who else knew?"

"Carter," Polly said.

"You told Carter Moody?" John looked at Laurel, confusion in his dark eyes.

"I...I...yes," Laurel said.

"Then it had to have been Moody." John knew for certain that the other man had been the informant, and he couldn't help but feel hurt that Laurel would have shared something so private with Carter.

"No," Laurel said still staring at John with blind eyes. "Carter would never do such a thing."

"And I would?" Pain shot through John like the hot edge of a branding iron. Dammit, how could she trust Carter when she didn't trust him? After all they'd shared, she should know he could never do anything to hurt her.

"Laurel, dear, I think John may be right," Polly said as she came to stand beside her niece.

"How can you say that?" Laurel looked at her aunt as if she were a stranger. "Carter knows what the biography means to me, what a scandal this could cause for our family. Of all people, he understands the importance of family pride and honor and . . . no, it wasn't Carter."

John wished that Laurel would stop sitting there staring at him as if he were an ax murderer. "If none of us told this . . . this Mabel person, then it had to have been Carter."

Laurel wondered how John could accuse Carter of such a thing, then she remembered that she had accused John. Oh, God, how could she think that John would do something so despicable? He loved her. They'd shared heaven together. She looked at John then, and tears filled her eyes.

Feeling a sense of panic, he grabbed Laurel by the shoulders and shook her gently. "Laurel, dammit all, it wasn't me."

"I don't want to believe it was you. My heart keeps telling me that it wasn't, but..." She looked at him, huge tears glistening in her eyes.

"It was Carter," John said, squeezing her shoulders, wanting to shake some sense into her. "Why would you rather believe me capable of such a thing than Carter?"

The telephone rang loudly, interrupting the tense conversation.

"I'll answer it in the parlor," Polly said, and left the kitchen.

"Carter isn't the kind of man who would do something like that." Laurel's gaze rested on the newspaper where John had tossed it onto the table.

"And I am? Is that what you're saying? I'm the man you profess to love, the man you spent the night with. I'm Johnny, remember. Your fantasy man, your Yankee lover." John released his hold on her and stood up. He'd been willing to accept the fact that he wasn't quite good enough for Laurel, that in her heart she might have him a little confused with the image of her dashing ancestor, but by God, he couldn't accept her lack of trust in him when she gave it to Carter Moody without question.

"Carter and I share a common heritage," Laurel said. "He's a man of integrity. He's a—"

"A Southern gentleman," John finished the sentence for her. "And what am I to you? Or better yet, who am I? I thought we made a commitment last night, a forever after kind of commitment. Was I wrong?"

Laurel couldn't answer him. She sat silently while tears cascaded down her flushed cheeks. We did make a forever after commitment, she wanted to tell him, but her lips refused to form the words. She loved John, but...but...dear Lord, she was so confused. She needed time to think.

"Just who did you make that commitment to, Laurel? Me or Johnny Drew's ghost?"

Laurel gasped, taking in quick, sobbing breaths. She tried to force herself to reply, but the words wouldn't come. She loved John Mason, not Johnny Drew, and she knew in her heart of hearts that John had not betrayed her, but somehow, she couldn't make her lips move.

"I'll tell you what, honey. When you decide whether you love me or your sainted ancestor and whether you trust me or not, give me a call." Angrily, John walked toward the hallway. "I'll be in Florida, soaking up sunshine and breathing some fresh air that isn't tainted by hundred-year-old ghosts."

With that said, John walked out the door and down the hall. Laurel sat in the kitchen chair, her face wet with tears, and the numbness cocooning her body slowly dissolved, leaving her in agonizing pain. By the time she forced her body to move, she heard the sound of John's car. She ran down the hallway and out the open front door.

"John! John . . . John. . . ." she cried his name into the wind, into the emptiness.

John Mason's car disappeared down the long driveway just as Polly Drew came out onto the front veranda.

"It's Bonnie Jean on the phone. I think you should talk to her."

"Not now."

"Yes, now."

Laurel turned around and faced her aunt, realizing that the older woman would not have insisted unless the matter was urgent.

Laurel went into the parlor and picked up the phone. "Bonnie Jean?"

"Laurel, you need to come over to my place right away. I've been trying forever to get through to you."

"What is it?" Laurel asked.

"C.J.'s here." Bonnie Jean paused. The silence on the line was deafening. "Wheeler was over here last night, and C.J. came here to find him. He was drunk as a skunk and spouting off some nonsense about your Pappy Drew. When he passed out, Wheeler asked me to let him stay. I realized what he was trying to tell his uncle when I saw the morning paper."

"I'll be right over." Laurel hung up the phone and turned to see Aunt Polly standing in the doorway.

"It was Carter, wasn't it?" her aunt asked.

"Yes, it was Carter," Laurel said.

Laurel's hand was unbelievably steady as she knocked loudly on the wooden door. It had taken her less than fifteen minutes to get from Aunt Polly's to Sugar Hill, but each mile had seemed like a hundred while she thought about the horrible minutes she'd spent in the kitchen with

John. Why had she been so willing to suspect him, to accuse him after he'd sworn his innocence? She didn't blame him for lashing out at her, for walking away and not looking back. She had allowed one more aspect of her snobbish upbringing to push her away from the man she loved. Somewhere deep inside, she'd been afraid to completely commit herself to John and a lifetime with him. But before she could face John and ask his forgiveness, she had to see Carter. If she couldn't trust Carter Moody, could she trust her heritage? Her way of life? Herself?

When the front door swung open, Bonnie Jean stepped outside onto the narrow porch. Laurel looked at the other woman and saw weariness and sympathy written plainly on her face. "Is he awake?" Laurel asked.

"Yeah." Bonnie Jean walked past Laurel and stood gazing down the tree-lined street in front of her neat little brick house. "I made him some fresh coffee. I told him you were on your way over."

"Exactly what happened?" Laurel turned around and stood beside Bonnie Jean, thinking how ironic that Carter had spent the night under the same roof with a woman he despised.

"Like I told you on the phone...C.J. came over here late last night trying to find Wheeler." Bonnie Jean looked at Laurel as if she were seeking understanding.

The last thing Laurel wanted right this minute was to make a moral judgement about Bonnie Jean's relationship with Carter's uncle. For years she'd chosen to consider the matter none of her business. "You said Carter was drunk and saying things about Pappy Drew?"

"He told Wheeler that you were in love with John Mason, and that he'd fixed you and your Yankee lover but good."

"Carter actually said that?" Laurel didn't want to believe a man she'd cared for and respected was capable of such an ignoble act. An action based on anything so primitive as emotion was totally out of character for Carter Moody.

"Look, Laurel, he was falling down drunk, and we both know C.J. isn't a drinking man. Wheeler loves him, and he was worried sick. Anyway, C.J. managed to blurt out bits and pieces about an old trunk and the diary and—"

"And the fact that my great-great-grandfather was a bigamist."

"Yeah, but we didn't pay much attention to that. When C.J. passed out, Wheeler thought it best for him to sleep it off on my couch."

"Which was quite a shock for him when he awakened, no doubt." Laurel smiled despite the gravity of her own situation because she hoped with all her heart that Carter felt ten times a fool when he came-to under Bonnie Jean's roof.

"As soon as I saw the paper this morning, I started trying to call you, but your line was dead. Look, you probably want to talk to C.J. alone, so I'll just take a little walk."

"No, don't go." Laurel grabbed Bonnie Jean's arm. "I have to hear him admit what he did. I need to understand how he could have done such a thing."

"It'll be twice as hard for him if I'm there."

"Good. I don't want to make this easy for him. Why should you?"

Bonnie Jean stared at Laurel, then nodded affirmatively. The two women entered the living room and found Carter, his usually immaculate clothes wrinkled, and his clean-shaven face covered with a day's growth of dark, heavy beard. He didn't even look like the Carter Jackson Moody IV that Laurel had known all her life. He looked haggard yet burly, withdrawn yet more manly than she'd ever seen him. His clear, blue eyes met hers in an honest stare of shame and remorse.

"Laurel . . . I . . . God, I'm sorry."

She braced herself against the door frame, half afraid she'd hit him and half afraid she'd take him in her arms as if he were a repentant child. "Why, Carter? Why?"

"Because I'm a fool. We were two of a kind, Laurel. Both of us trapped by our noble heritage. But you were going to escape." He stood perfectly still, his unsteady hands clutching the ends of his open shirt where it swung freely on each side of his hips.

"I don't understand. How could you, of all people, destroy everything my family has stood for, everything I believed in?

"Damnation! What do you think I am? I'm a man just like your Yankee. I feel. I hurt. I make mistakes."

Laurel looked at Carter as if she'd never seen him before in her life, for indeed the man standing in front of her was a stranger. What had happened to that suave, austere Southern gentleman who'd always treated her as if she were made of spun glass? "Do you realize that you've destroyed any hope I ever had of getting Pappy Drew's biography published? Your interview with Mabel Suggs has destroyed a legend."

"Good." Carter said with conviction, his voice strong but quiet. "You and I have spent our whole lives drowning in ancestor worship. We've played our parts to the hilt. Hell, we were perfect for each other. The perfect gentleman and his lady. The whole county thought it was inevitable that we marry and produce another generation of Alabama blue bloods. But there was one slight problem for you, wasn't there?"

Laurel looked across the room at Bonnie Jean who stood quietly behind the couch, trying to be as inconspicuous as possible.

"When we touched, when we kissed, nothing happened," Carter said, a mask of rigid strength beginning to conceal his emotions. "We left each other cold. But what the hell. You didn't care. You had your fantasy lover to fulfill your needs, didn't you?''

Laurel knew she couldn't deny his accusations. "What...what about you? You never said a word, never let on that it mattered.''

Carter snorted, shaking his head in self-disgust. "It didn't matter. I don't need fireworks—chemistry—sexual attraction. Not me. Not Carter Jackson Moody IV. Hell, I married a woman handpicked for me by my mother and my aunt and spent years in a sterile, loveless marriage. I cared a lot more about you than I ever did about Kathie Lou.''

"What does your loveless marriage and our lack of a real relationship have to do with why you told Mabel Suggs about the diary?''

"You honestly don't know, do you?''

"No, I don't.''

"Because..." Carter snapped his head around and glared at Bonnie Jean whose eyes were filled with tears. "You're enjoying this aren't you, Bonnie Jean? You're just waiting to hear me say it.''

"Carter!" Laurel's harsh voice shifted his attention back to her.

"For just a little while, a few stupid hours, I hated you because...because I saw everything you felt for that damned Yankee in your eyes when you told me you loved him. You were going to be free, to have it all, and I was going to be left with nothing...again. Once, years ago...I... Never mind. What I did was stupid. I punished you for a lifetime of my own mistakes.''

"Oh, dear Lord," Laurel cried. "I've got to use your phone. I've got to call John.''

"If you want privacy—" Bonnie Jean said.

"No, I..." Laurel grabbed the phone sitting on the end table by the couch while Bonnie Jean and Carter watched her dial the number.

"Connect me with room 118," Laurel said. "What? When? Oh. Thank you." She hung up the phone and stood there staring down at it, her hand trembling where it still clutched the receiver.

"Laurel, are you all right?" Bonnie Jean asked.

"John's gone," Laurel said. "He checked out."

"Didn't he leave a message?" Bonnie Jean walked toward Laurel, never once looking at Carter.

Laurel felt very light-headed, and the room seemed to swirl around her, but she was determined to walk out of the house on her own two feet. She released her tight grip on the phone and faced Bonnie Jean. "Yes, he left a message. He delivered it to me personally before he left this morning."

Laurel took three tentative steps toward the front door, swayed slightly, then crumpled to the floor in a dead faint.

Twelve

————

Are you sure you've got everything?'' Polly Drew asked her niece as they stood beside the open trunk of her Riviera.

Laurel clasped the small suitcase in one hand while trying to adjust her lightweight shoulder bag with the other. "Yes, I'm sure. After all, I have no idea how long I'll be staying. John may very well send me straight back home. And who could blame him after the shameful way I treated him?''

"Nonsense," Polly said as she closed the car trunk. "I'm not expecting you back until you two come for a visit as man and wife.''

Laurel and her aunt walked toward the airport terminal. "I could have driven you to Huntsville, and you could have taken a direct flight.''

Laurel pushed open the glass doors and walked inside. "Go sit down while I confirm my reservation.''

Muttering under her breath, Polly stalked off. Laurel smiled, shaking her head. During the last two weeks since John had left and the whole world had learned the truth about Pappy Drew, Aunt Polly had been Laurel's lifeline. It was her aunt's prodding that gave her the courage to call Nate Hodges and obtain his assistance. Oddly enough, the man seemed delighted to fill her in on John's activities, his loneliness, and his lack of female companionship. When Nate told her to get her fanny down to St. Augustine before his old buddy threw himself into the ocean, she knew it wasn't too late. For some wonderful reason, fate had decided to give her a second chance. And she meant to take that chance, even if it meant crawling on her hands and knees to beg John's forgiveness.

The horrible day she'd discovered Carter's betrayal, she'd been certain her life was over, her dreams ended, and the one man she loved lost to her forever. But as day slowly, painfully, evolved into night and back into a new day, Laurel began to put the pieces of her broken life together. But the important piece was missing. When she'd worked through the disillusionment, the embarrassment, and the lost dreams, Laurel realized that she loved and trusted John Mason. He had offered her fulfillment of the most important dream, the most cherished hope, and she'd been too blind to see, too wrapped up in a girl's fantasy to appreciate a woman's reality.

It had taken time and deep soul-searching for Laurel to come to terms with her life, past, present and future. She supposed Carter had done her an enormous favor in acting so out of character. By having to face the truth about Johnny Drew, she was better able to understand everything about her whole life, all the pretenses, the lies, the illusions. Whether a man was a Yankee or a Southerner, a gentleman or a roughneck, had nothing to do with his worth as a human being or his capacity for love. She decided that there was nothing wrong with dreams as long as you didn't allow them to distort reality.

The one thing Laurel Drew knew without a doubt was that she wanted to spend the rest of her life with a big, blond ex-sailor who knew absolutely nothing about being a Southern gentleman and everything about being a man. Now, all she had to do was go to Florida, confront John, and hope he loved her enough to forgive her.

Laurel left the ticket desk and sat down beside her aunt, laying the suitcase and bag on an adjoining chair. "My flight leaves in twenty minutes."

"Is this Nate person going to pick you up at the airport?" Polly snapped open her purse and rummaged around inside as if looking for something.

"No. I'm going to call him when I get there, and he's going to give me instructions on how to get to his house." Laurel watched in fascination as Polly took several objects out of her large purse and lay them in her lap.

"So you'll see John and the two of you will work out all your problems." The elderly woman kept digging through the assortment of items in her large leather handbag, obviously distracted by not being able to immediately find the object of her hunt.

"For heaven's sake, Aunt Polly, what are you looking for?" Laurel laughed.

"Thank goodness. Here it is." Polly pulled her hand out of the bag and opened her palm to reveal a small silver box. "I want you to give this to John on your wedding day."

Laurel looked down, her eyes riveted to the tiny box as her aunt opened the lid. There, nestled on the aged white velvet, was a man's gold ring. "This was my William's and his father's before him."

"Aunt Polly, no." Laurel knew immediately that the antique ring had been Johnny Drew's wedding band, handed down to the eldest son in each generation.

Polly lay the open box in her lap and gazed down at the delicate diamond and amethyst ring she wore beside her own wedding band. "This ring is its mate." Polly slipped the ring off her finger and put it in the box on top of the man's ring. "For you and John."

"No. Please, no. I can't take these. It's so wonderful of you to offer them to me, but John would never understand. He'd think...I...I don't ever want him to think that I've got him confused with Clarice's Yankee lover."

"Oh, he's probably over all that nonsense by now. Anyway, since William and I were never blessed with children, who better then Clarice and Johnny's great-great-granddaughter and J. T. Andrews's great-great-great-nephew to have these rings? Besides, you'll want your children to have them someday."

Polly closed the silver box and handed it to her niece. Laurel hesitated briefly, then took the box and held it against her heart as she shut her eyes, praying that she would have the chance to give John a child.

The St. Augustine sky and the Atlantic Ocean embraced in a rhapsody of blue and white. Early morning sunlight bathed the beach, turning the sand into tawny diamond particles. John Mason walked alone behind Nate Hodges's house. Every morning during the last two weeks, he'd left his bed at dawn to walk by the ocean and think about Laurel. In the moments of solitude he found in these daily strolls, he'd been able to find peace within himself and a determination to wait for the woman he loved to make the first move. It wasn't stubbornness on his part, but a certain knowledge that the only way he and Laurel could have a life together was if she could lay all her ghosts to rest and come to him free and ready to love and trust.

"Hey," a deep baritone voice called out. "Coffee."

John waved an acknowledgement to his friend Nate and turned toward the small enclosed patio at the rear of the stucco house.

Nate Hodges handed John a mug, swung one long leg over and straddled a patio chair. "Why the hell don't you go get her?"

"Dammit, man, will you let it be," John said, clutching the mug in his hand and looking down into the steaming liquid. "If I go after her, it'll prove nothing to either of us. She's the one who didn't trust me, the one who didn't believe in what we had together."

"What are you going to do if Laurel doesn't come to you? This town is full of good-looking women." Nate took a large gulp of coffee.

"I'm not interested."

"Are you ready to forgive her if she does come down here looking for you?"

"You're as nosy as an old woman, Hodges." John raised his mug to his lips and sipped, savoring the taste of his buddy's good coffee. "You're one of the few men I know who can make a decent cup of coffee."

"Look, John, I've given you a lot of space since you've been here. I haven't pressed you about anything personal. Hell, I haven't even demanded that you make a definite decision about going into business with me."

"So why all the questions this morning?" John took a cigarette from the pack lying on the glass patio table. "You've been acting funny the last couple of days. It wouldn't have anything to do with those mysterious phone calls, would it?"

"I told you it was a woman. Hey, you know how it is." Nate chuckled that smug, macho laugh that one man gives another when he's saying "I know her well."

"So you said." John sat down in a chaise longue on the opposite side of the patio.

"I've known you for seventeen years, John, and I've never seen you so bent out of shape over a woman."

"Okay. Okay. I'll give her another week, and if she hasn't got in touch with me, I'm going back to Alabama to get her."

"Whoa . . . what are you going to do, kidnap her if she doesn't want to leave the old plantation?"

"Something like that."

"How the mighty have fallen," Nate said, mocking a forlorn sigh. "I can remember the good old days when you loved 'em and left 'em all over the world."

"Why don't you go take a dip in the ocean?"

"I've got a better suggestion—" The sound of the door-bell echoing through the open patio doors interrupted the conversation.

John started to get up, but Nate motioned him back down. "You go take a dip. I'll see who it is, get rid of them, and head on down to the marina."

"You expecting company this early? Your mysterious lady friend?" John lay back in the chaise longue.

Nate grinned and walked into the house, leaving John sipping leisurely on his morning coffee and enjoying his cigarette.

John lay there thinking about Nate's comment about the past. He guessed the two of them had sowed a few wild oats together. But just as he'd done over the last few years, Nate had slowed down a little, drank less, and sampled ladies' charms with more discernment. As far as John knew, Nate had never been seriously involved with a woman in the years they'd been friends. John wondered exactly who this mystery woman was. Nate had been as closemouthed as a clam, but John could tell by the look in his friend's cool, green eyes that the lady was someone special. Finding that one special woman could sure change a man's life.

Why hadn't Laurel come to him? he wondered. Why hadn't she at least called and told him she wanted to work things out? It had taken all his strength and determination to give her time . . . time to make her own decisions without the pressure his presence would have put on her. If he'd stayed in Tuscumbia, he wouldn't have stayed away from her. He could offer his love, but he couldn't make her dreams come true. He couldn't replace the fantasies he'd destroyed. She had to be willing to accept reality.

It had killed him to leave her, even as hurt and angry as he'd been. But he knew that for once Laurel had to find the courage to accept life the way it was and not the way she dreamed it should be. She couldn't have him *and* Johnny Drew. If she was half the woman he thought she was, she'd choose a less than perfect flesh and blood man who could make her body sing, over the legendary hero who'd been an illusion.

He'd told Nate that he'd wait another week for Laurel to come to him. Yeah, well, he doubted he could stand another day without her, let alone another week. His life was on standstill. Laurel was the only thing that mattered. She possessed his thoughts. She haunted his dreams. His body ached with the sweet memory of loving her, of holding her in his arms and whispering her name against her naked flesh. His soul cried out with loneliness, and he felt certain that her soul could hear those cries.

Laurel stepped through the open sliding glass doors and stood on the patio looking at John. He lay on the chaise longue, his big body long and hard and tempting. The morning sun, already summertime hot, wrapped his body in bright, clear light. His skimpy T-shirt was cut short in front, revealing the golden brown curls adorning his trim stomach. His eyes were closed, but she knew he wasn't asleep. Was he thinking of her? she wondered. Of the last time they'd made love? Or the last time they'd seen each other? She wanted to run to him, to go down on her knees and wrap her arms around him.

"John." Her voice was a mere whisper.

His whole body stiffened at the sound of the familiar voice, but he didn't open his eyes or acknowledge her presence in any way. He knew he'd heard Laurel call his name, but then it wasn't the first time in the last two weeks she'd called to him. He wanted her to be there with him so badly, he was imagining things.

"John." Her voice grew louder.

His eyes flew open, and he looked up to see what he thought was a mirage standing a few feet away. "Laurel?"

"Yes, it's me. I..."

He lay there looking at her, afraid to believe his own eyes, certain that if he closed and reopened them, she'd be gone. "Laurel?"

She took several steps toward him, her hands nervously clutching the sides of her white slacks. "I...I have to know if...if it's too late."

He sat up slowly, his black eyes riveted to her face as he dropped his cigarette onto the brick floor. "How'd you know where...did you call Nate?"

His questions stopped her steady progression across the patio. "I called Nate two days ago to see if you were here, and he...well, he told me to get my fanny down here fast."

John smiled as he realized that Laurel was the mystery woman with whom his old friend had shared the very private telephone conversations. "Did he tell you that he's been on the verge of having me committed? God, Laurel, I've been going crazy."

She felt tears stinging her eyes and joy bursting within her heart. It isn't too late, it really isn't, she told herself as she took several more steps toward John.

"Can you ever forgive me for doubting you? Oh, John, I knew in my heart you could never betray me. I...I know now that I let my fears and prejudices come between us."

He sat there and looked at her without saying a word. He had a right to hear her beg a little, he thought. Didn't he? But he didn't want to see her humble herself. She'd already punished herself enough. All he wanted was her.

"I despise myself for hurting you the way I did. Please, John. Please...."

He stood up then, opened his arms, and held them out to her. She rushed into his welcoming embrace, flinging her arms around his neck and burying her face against his chest.

"What took you so long, woman?" he asked huskily, his lips brushing her forehead and his arms tightening around her.

"Why didn't you stay in Tuscumbia?"

"I couldn't. I had to give you the time and space to make your own decisions."

"Why didn't you call?"

"Why didn't you?"

"I've missed you, John. I wanted to call every day that we've been apart, but I wasn't sure of myself and of what I could and couldn't give up."

"Are you sure now?" His hands roamed her body, renewing an acquaintance with the soft contours tormenting his manhood.

"Yes, I'm sure. You're all I want. All I'll ever want. If you can forgive me and let me have another chance, I promise I'll—"

His lips hovered over her hers, and she wanted nothing more than to taste him, to feel his mouth cover hers, but once that happened the talking would end and the loving would begin. She wanted, no, she needed to tell him so many things before they gave in to temptation.

She covered his lips with her fingers. "Carter gave the story about Pappy Drew to the *Colbert Daily News*. The day you left, he confessed. Oh, John, please forgive me for ever doubting you."

John sat down on the chaise longue, pulled her onto his lap, and held her against his body. "Oh, honey, you don't know how that hurt. When you trusted him more than you did me, it was like having a knife slice my heart out."

"Carter was a part of the mythical world I'd created for myself. I saw him and my father and Uncle William sort of like knights in shining armor. The kind of man I thought Johnny Drew was. I'm not sure the type of Southern gentleman I fantasized ever really existed. But you, John

Mason, are exactly the kind of Yankee lover I want, the kind Grandmother Clarice had.''

''Laurel, I'm not Johnny Drew. I'm not—''

''I know exactly who you are and who you aren't. You, like J. T. Andrews, are a man. Real and honest and sexy as hell. You don't make pretty speeches, and you don't have perfect manners, but when we look at each other, when we touch each other, I feel so wonderful inside, so happy, so... so loved. I want that man... and that bonding that comes from physical desire yet goes beyond it to unite our souls.''

John unbuttoned the top two buttons of her blouse and placed his lips against the pulse in her throat. ''Right now, all I can think about is the physical. Later, after I've been deep inside you, filling you, completing you as you complete me, we'll talk about spiritual and eternal.''

He smiled at her, and her stomach quivered with excitement. She loved his smile, his oh so familiar smile that had always reminded her of Johnny Drew's. She touched his lips with her fingertips.

''I used to look at your mouth and see Johnny Drew's smile. I thought that was part of my confusion.''

John tried not to frown, but he did when a wave of fear engulfed him. ''I thought you said—''

She covered his mouth with her fingers. ''It's your smile I love, and the reason I kept seeing Johnny Drew's when I looked at you is because your mouths are identical.''

John looked puzzled. ''What?''

''Genes, my darling. Heredity. Somehow you inherited your great uncle J.T.'s mouth.''

John laughed with relief and hugged her closer within his possessive arms.

''I'm going to rewrite Johnny Drew's biography,'' Laurel told him as he finished unbuttoning her blouse. ''I thought that now I've quit my job as a history teacher and will be spending all my time lounging around on the beaches here in St. Augustine—"

"You quit your job?" His fingers hesitated at the front catch of her bra.

"I'm going to write the true account of Clarice DuBois's Yankee lover. Do you think my Yankee lover can support me while I complete the book?" Laurel slipped her hands up and underneath John's T-shirt, her fingers raking through the thick swirls of chest hair.

"Are you saying that you'd marry me and live here in Florida?" His dark eyes searched hers for the answer, happiness filling his heart at the look of love he saw on her face.

"Are you asking me?" She ran her tongue up the side of his neck.

"Marry me, Laurel. I'm not a rich man, but I'm going into business with Nate, and I'll be able to take care of you."

"Well I'm not a rich woman, you know, but I do think I'll eventually be able to find a teaching job down here. I guess I could take care of you, too."

John laughed as his fingers released her bra snap. "I love you, Laurel. I love you in a way I never knew existed."

"And I love you, John. My Johnny, flesh and blood and all man."

His heart swelled with love and pride. What he felt for Laurel and she felt for him was love in every sense of the word. He realized that he wanted it all . . . the physical, the mental, the spiritual. This was forever.

With tender, loving hands, John undressed Laurel. Her blouse, her bra, her sandals, her slacks, and her panties disappeared one at a time, revealing more and more of her luscious flesh to his eyes and mouth. Not one inch of her body was left untouched. Laurel made no protest when he slid her beneath him on the chaise longue, then slipped down her body, his lips savoring the slow, sensual journey. When his knees touched the floor, he took her foot in his hands, gently massaging. His lips touched her ankle. His tongue tormented the side of her calf as it stroked upward to the inside of her thighs. The loving continued, drawing closer and closer to her heat, and John thought surely he would catch fire from the flame of passion burning so brightly within her.

"I love the taste of you," he said, his hands reaching upward to take her breasts. "And the feel of you. God, honey, there's never been anyone like you . . . never."

Laurel grasped his shoulders when his fingers found the sensitive peaks of her breasts and his mouth moved over her, teasing, promising, yet not fulfilling. Flashes of heat spiraled out from her breasts, spread through her stomach, and caught fire between her legs. And she burned.

"Please, John . . . please."

"Open up for me, Laurel. Give me what I want. Let me love you."

In a moment of complete trust, Laurel gave herself to John, and in return, he loved her with an intimacy that told her the depths of his desire for her, the capacity within him to give pleasure before seeking his own.

John clutched her hips, bringing her closer, reveling in the taste and scent of the woman he loved as one final stroke of his tongue carried her over the edge into a chasm of earth-shattering ecstasy. As her body trembled with release, she plunged her fingers through his hair, clinging to the blond strands as she moaned his name over and over again.

John pulled away from Laurel long enough to divest himself of his shorts, T-shirt and briefs. "You're beautiful," he said, looking at her naked body and glowing face as she lay there with a seductive smile beckoning him to share the joy with her this time.

"I want you . . . inside me. I ache with emptiness." Her knees brushed the sides of his ribs, urging him to move up and over her.

"You're everything . . . to me." He held himself poised above her, his manhood against the threshold of her femininity. He probed. She arched and accepted him and they both cried from the rapture, the sheer pleasure of joining. He lay nestled within her, unmoving, savoring the feel of her body holding his in the most intimate caress male and female can share. "I want you so much, I'm afraid I'll hurt you," he told her, his mouth nuzzling at her earlobe.

"You could never hurt me when I want you as much as you want me." She tightened around him, released, and tightened again, her body speaking to his in a language as old as time.

"But you're so delicate, so fragile."

Laurel sought his mouth with her own and claimed his lips in a kiss of temptation. Her hands soothed the tenseness she found in his back and waist and buttocks. When her fingers moved around his hips, exploring the minute space that separated them, John groaned in an agony of desire. When she cupped him tenderly, fondling the source of his virility, she whispered a woman's words of enticement.

"Oh...baby...yes." His body jerked, once, twice, and then he began a heated dance of passion, his manhood plunging into her hard and fast, with an urgency to which she responded equally. He gave. She took. He took. She gave. Harder and faster, hotter and wilder, he thrust into her as sensation after sensation coursed through her until waves of unbearable pleasure washed over her. Her cries of fulfillment blended with the sound of the morning surf kissing the shore.

"So hot...so good." John mumbled against her lips as his tongue surged into her mouth and his life-giving love poured into her receptive body.

"I love you," Laurel said, holding him possessively, while satisfaction claimed their passion-wet bodies.

"Love you...Laurel...forever."

Epilogue

One week later, in a small, very private ceremony, John Andrews Mason and Laurel Clarice Drew exchanged antique rings and vowed to love, honor, and cherish all the days of their lives. They knew they could never be happier than they were on their wedding day, but Polly Drew and Dora Jansen, with the wisdom of age, predicted far greater happiness in the future. And they were right. Exactly nine months and two days after John and Laurel made love on Nate's patio, Johnny Drew Mason made his debut into the world. A big, beautiful baby with his mother's violet eyes, his father's golden hair, and a legacy of love over a century old.

* * * * *

Back by popular demand, some of Diana Palmer's earliest published books are available again!

Several years ago, Diana Palmer began her writing career. Sweet, compelling and totally unforgettable, these are the love stories that enchanted readers everywhere.

Next month, six more of these wonderful stories will be available in DIANA PALMER DUETS—Books 4, 5 and 6. Each DUET contains two powerful stories plus an introduction by Diana Palmer. Don't miss:

Book Four   **AFTER THE MUSIC**
                        DREAM'S END

Book Five   **BOUND BY A PROMISE**
                        PASSION FLOWER

Book Six   **TO HAVE AND TO HOLD**
                        THE COWBOY AND THE LADY

DPD-1

SILHOUETTE'S "BIG WIN"
SWEEPSTAKES RULES & REGULATIONS
NO PURCHASE NECESSARY TO ENTER OR RECEIVE A PRIZE

1. To enter and join the Reader Service, scratch off the metallic strips on all your BIG WIN tickets #1-#6. This will reveal the values for each sweepstakes entry number, the number of free book(s) you will receive, and your free bonus gift as part of our Reader Service. If you do not wish to take advantage of our Reader Service, but wish to enter the Sweepstakes only, scratch off the metallic strips on your BIG WIN tickets #1-#4. Return your entire sheet of tickets intact. Incomplete and/or inaccurate entries are ineligible for that section or sections of prizes. Not responsible for mutilated or unreadable entries or inadvertent printing errors. Mechanically reproduced entries are null and void.

2. Whether you take advantage of this offer or not, your Sweepstakes numbers will be compared against a list of winning numbers generated at random by the computer. In the event that all prizes are not claimed by March 31, 1992, a random drawing will be held from all qualified entries received from March 30, 1990 to March 31, 1992, to award all unclaimed prizes. All cash prizes (Grand to Sixth), will be mailed to the winners and are payable by cheque in U.S. funds. Seventh prize to be shipped to winners via third-class mail. These prizes are in addition to any free, surprise or mystery gifts that might be offered. Versions of this sweepstakes with different prizes of approximately equal value may appear in other mailings or at retail outlets by Torstar Corp. and its affiliates.

3. The following prizes are awarded in this sweepstakes: ★ Grand Prize (1) $1,000,000; First Prize (1) $35,000; Second Prize (1) $10,000; Third Prize (5) $5,000; Fourth Prize (10) $1,000; Fifth Prize (100) $250; Sixth Prize (2500) $10; ★ ★ Seventh Prize (6000) $12.95 ARV.

   ★ This Sweepstakes contains a Grand Prize offering of $1,000,000 annuity. Winner will receive $33,333.33 a year for 30 years without interest totalling $1,000,000.

   ★ ★ Seventh Prize: A fully illustrated hardcover book published by Torstar Corp. Approximate value of the book is $12.95.

   Entrants may cancel the Reader Service at any time without cost or obligation to buy (see details in center insert card).

4. This promotion is being conducted under the supervision of Marden-Kane, Inc., an independent judging organization. By entering this Sweepstakes, each entrant accepts and agrees to be bound by these rules and the decisions of the judges, which shall be final and binding. Odds of winning in the random drawing are dependent upon the total number of entries received. Taxes, if any, are the sole responsibility of the winners. Prizes are nontransferable. All entries must be received by no later than 12:00 NOON, on March 31, 1992. The drawing for all unclaimed sweepstakes prizes will take place May 30, 1992, at 12:00 NOON, at the offices of Marden-Kane, Inc., Lake Success, New York.

5. This offer is open to residents of the U.S., the United Kingdom, France and Canada, 18 years or older except employees and their immediate family members of Torstar Corp., its affiliates, subsidiaries, Marden-Kane, Inc., and all other agencies and persons connected with conducting this Sweepstakes. All Federal, State and local laws apply. Void wherever prohibited or restricted by law. Any litigation respecting the conduct and awarding of a prize in this publicity contest may be submitted to the Régie des loteries et courses du Québec.

6. Winners will be notified by mail and may be required to execute an affidavit of eligibility and release which must be returned within 14 days after notification or, an alternative winner will be selected. Canadian winners will be required to correctly answer an arithmetical skill-testing question administered by mail which must be returned within a limited time. Winners consent to the use of their names, photographs and/or likenesses for advertising and publicity in conjunction with this and similar promotions without additional compensation.

7. For a list of major winners, send a stamped, self-addressed envelope to: WINNERS LIST, c/o MARDEN-KANE, INC., P.O. BOX 701, SAYREVILLE, NJ 08871. Winners Lists will be fulfilled after the May 30, 1992 drawing date.

If Sweepstakes entry form is missing, please print your name and address on a 3" × 5" piece of plain paper and send to:

In the U.S.
Silhouette's "BIG WIN" Sweepstakes
901 Fuhrmann Blvd.
P.O. Box 1867
Buffalo, NY 14269-1867

In Canada
Silhouette's "BIG WIN" Sweepstakes
P.O. Box 609
Fort Erie, Ontario
L2A 5X3

Offer limited to one per household.

LTY-S790RR

Diamond Jubilee Collection

It's our 10th Anniversary...
and *you* get a present!

This collection of early Silhouette
Romances features novels written
by three of your favorite authors:

ANN MAJOR—*Wild Lady*
ANNETTE BROADRICK—*Circumstantial Evidence*
DIXIE BROWNING—*Island on the Hill*

* These Silhouette Romance titles were first published in the early 1980s
  and have not been available since!

* Beautiful Collector's Edition bound in antique green simulated leather to
  last a lifetime!

* Embossed in gold on the cover and spine!

This special collection will not be sold in retail stores and is only available
through this exclusive offer.
Look for details in all Silhouette series published in June, July and August.